THE MAGIC HOUR

MIA KENT

The Magic Hour

By Mia Kent

Be the first to know about new releases! Sign up for my newsletter here. Your information will never be shared.

CHAPTER 1

Daphne Hall wrapped her arms around her body as the ferry churned to life and began chugging away from the Dolphin Bay harbor. The breeze off the ocean had kicked up, dropping the temperature by several degrees, but the tourists were undeterred—as the ferry passed the island's golden-sand beaches, Daphne could see a steady stream of vacationers making their way to shore, their arms weighed down with umbrellas and chairs, the little ones dragging sand toys, kites, and boogie boards.

Even though many of Dolphin Bay's year-round residents enjoyed the summer months, when the island was bustling and business was booming, Daphne preferred the quiet solitude that settled over the shores at winter—mainly because that meant a few months of less taxing workdays. Sal's Diner was the island hotspot for residents and tourists alike, and the more crowded the beaches got, the more frazzled Daphne and the rest of the staff became. Sal, the hot-tempered, big-bellied man who owned and operated the diner, looked to be on the verge of a perpetual heart attack from Memorial Day through Labor Day, and on more than one occasion, Daphne had eyed his red face and manic expression with alarm, one finger on her cell phone's emergency button.

Luckily, Daphne thought, stretching her legs out in front of her and settling into her seat as the ferry kicked up sea spray around her, today was her day off—a rare occurrence during the height of tourist season. Unluckily, she was spending it with her sister.

Corinne was everything Daphne wasn't—confident, successful, a go-getter with a picture-perfect life, which included a handsome husband who doted on her and, more recently—and the reason for Daphne's long-overdue visit—a new baby. When she found out that Corinne was expecting, Daphne had celebrated with her like any big sister should—she helped organize the shower, oohed and aahed with her over tiny outfits at the department store, listened on the phone while Corinne endlessly debated baby names—but at every turn, she felt like she was going through the motions, performing the tasks she was expected to perform with as much enthusiasm as she could muster, none of it real.

She loved her sister, she did. But ever since Corinne had left the island, Daphne had always felt… lesser… in her presence. Like she wasn't quite good enough. Successful enough. Smart enough. Attractive enough.

Just… not enough.

Corinne could never understand why Daphne had stayed on the island, where job opportunities were scarce and she saw the same faces, day in and day out, for years on end, while the rest of the world passed her by.

Daphne could never understand how her sister had left their mother behind without a second thought.

It was a wedge that was driven between them deeply, would perhaps always be lurking on the outskirts of their relationship, making true connection, true sisterhood, impossible.

At least she had Tana.

Daphne smiled as she thought of her friend who

was quickly becoming family. Although they had been summer best friends throughout their childhood, Tana had left for college and then the West Coast, and more than twenty years had passed since they had seen each other, or even spoken, outside of a few perfunctory phone calls and holiday cards that had gradually tapered off to nothing. Recently, though, Tana had returned to the island to help care for her aging great-uncle—and also to escape the heartbreak of her recent separation from her husband—and she and Daphne had picked up right where they'd left off all those years ago.

Daphne was thrilled to have Tana back in her life, and she was even more thrilled that her friend seemed to be on the cusp of finding love again. Reed was a wonderful man, as steady and solid as they came, and the two of them had their first date just last night—a romantic dinner by the sea that Daphne had helped orchestrate.

She'd been happy to do it, but she couldn't help the nagging, hollow feeling it opened up inside her, the same loneliness she felt every time she turned off her lights at night and settled in to sleep next to her cat, Luna, who always seemed rather lukewarm about her presence. Years had passed since Daphne had been in a relationship, and even longer still since she'd been in love.

No. Don't think about him.

Daphne straightened in her seat and gazed out over the blue-gray waters as the purple outline of the mainland in the distance began to grow clearer. It had been a long time since she'd let Jax Keller get under her skin, and she wasn't about to allow him to creep in now, when her defenses were down and she was already dreading what the day would bring.

Tana's return to the island brought with it the inevitable memories of those sun-drenched summer days and gossamer nights, when Daphne and Jax had stayed on the beach as the night sky lightened to a purple twilight, their hands entwined as they gazed up at the stars, the rise and fall of their chests in sync as their friendship deepened to something much more, something that both left an indelible print on her heart and almost broke her in two.

For the past few weeks, Daphne had slammed the door on each memory as it resurfaced, leaving behind only the hazy outline of teenage promises that had been left unfulfilled, of heartbreak so real and visceral she could almost taste it on the air.

She had only been seventeen. But oh, how she'd loved him, without condition or reservation, the kind of love that was pure in its innocence and naïve in its belief that it would last forever.

Because he'd said he loved her too. He'd promised her the world—with the kind of happily-ever-afters that a young girl from a broken home clings to with everything she has, every ounce of hope she can muster.

He'd said that he would rescue her.

He'd lied.

∼

"DAPHNE! I'm so glad you're finally here."

Corinne opened her arms in welcome, then pulled her sister into a limp pseudo-hug before air-kissing her on both cheeks. Then she stepped back and eyed the wrapped packages in Daphne's arms.

"A gift? You didn't have to do that. I'm sure you're barely making ends meet at the diner. If you want to return them, it's okay with me. We've been absolutely *spoiling* Harper; she's got just about everything a one-month-old needs to make it through the day. Our nanny says she's never seen such a well-stocked nursery, and she used to work for the mayor."

Corinne's voice was smug as she fingered the string of pearls around her neck. When she turned at the sound of an infant crying somewhere in the palatial house, Daphne snagged the opportunity to take three deep, calming breaths before plastering a tight smile on her face and practically shoving the gifts into her sister's arms.

"Don't worry, I'll manage to scrape up a hunk of bread and a lump of cheese for my dinner," she retorted, following Corinne into the house, which somehow looked to have grown even larger since the last time she'd visited.

"Yes, we hired a contractor to complete some renovations on the old place," Corinne said, noticing her glancing around. "We added an attached apartment for our live-in nanny so she'll feel more comfortable... and Raymond and I don't have to spend our evenings entertaining her," she added in a semi-whisper as Daphne trailed after her. She couldn't help noticing her sister's svelte figure and perfectly made-up face—Daphne had never been blessed with children of her own, but she'd seen other new moms, and, well, "put-together" wasn't usually the description of them that normally came to mind.

"How's Harper?" Daphne asked. They entered the living room, which was stylishly decorated in soft whites and creams, and she immediately noticed the lack of infant swings, toys, or even an errant diaper. Her own small apartment was far messier, and the only person she shared it with was a cat who only appeared at mealtimes.

"Oh, she's an absolute *handful.*" Corinne led Daphne into the expansive dining room, where a set of sparkling glasses were arranged around a crystal pitcher filled with iced tea. A tray of tea sandwiches sat nearby, each cut into a perfect triangle and stuffed with cucumber and cream cheese filling.

"Our nanny reported that she was up most of the night—she barely got a wink of sleep." Corinne yawned widely and patted the skin beneath her eyes. "Much more of this and I'm going to need a visit to the spa, and what new mother has time for that?"

Here came the tinkling laughter again, and Daphne gritted her teeth against it, focusing instead on the tea sandwiches. She had worked the early morning shift at the diner before boarding the ferry, and she'd barely had time to scarf down a home-made strawberry muffin—one of the many recipes she was testing for the inn's grand reopening—before running out the door. She loaded several sandwiches onto a plate, and was in the process of lifting one to her lips and preparing to take a bite when she caught Corinne's sharp gaze—first on her face, and then roaming down to her stomach.

"What?" she asked, frowning at her sister and then down at the sandwich. "I just assumed it was okay for me to have one."

"It is, honey, it *is*." Corinne clasped her hands together in front of her trim waist. "I was just noticing how much you have Mom's figure, that's all."

As usual, the mention of their mother caused a knot to form in Daphne's stomach. She set the plate on the table, then folded her arms over her chest and squared off against her sister. "Do you mean Mom before she began drinking herself to death, or after?"

After their father had abandoned their mother—and them, by association—in favor of his secretary, Ruby Hall had gone from being a beautiful, vivacious woman with a laugh so big it filled every room to a depressed, haunted shell of a person who could barely raise herself out of bed. So most days, she didn't.

Daphne had taken it upon herself to care for her —washing her, buying her groceries, cooking for her, taking care of her bills, forcing her to go out and get some fresh air at least once a week. She'd taken on their mother's heartbreak as her own, but even that hadn't been enough to save her.

And while Daphne was up to her eyeballs in debt and despair, Corinne was busy on the mainland finding a rich husband. Their wedding had been a lavish affair, attended by some of the state's most well-connected people, but Daphne and Ruby, sitting by themselves at a table in the corner of the ballroom watching the guests schmooze, had felt like outcasts. Corinne didn't speak a word to them all night, other than to briefly introduce them to her new husband's parents, barely making eye contact as she hurried her wealthy in-laws away at the first opportunity.

"Come on, Daph," Corinne said, shaking a finger in her direction. "This is supposed to be a nice day, and you're here to see your niece for the first time. Do we really have to ruin it by talking about what our mother did to herself?"

And there it was, yet again. Her sister's lack of sympathy—of basic *humanity*—was never short of astounding to Daphne. It was the reason why she kept her distance, the reason why she'd been dreading this day since she got the phone call announcing her niece's arrival.

She opened her mouth to offer a retort but was

interrupted by a middle-aged woman entering the room, a tiny bundle of blankets in her arms.

"Here she is," Corinne cooed, taking the baby from the nanny before turning to Daphne. "Harper Grace Princeton, may I introduce you to your Auntie Daphne?"

Corinne passed the baby to Daphne, and she could feel her anger melting away as she gazed down at her niece's precious face—her perfect, tiny, upturned nose, gray-green eyes, and a shock of jet-black hair that was smoothed off her face by a frilly white headband. "Oh, Corinne," Daphne breathed, cuddling Harper in her arms and inhaling her new-baby scent. "She's absolutely perfect."

As Daphne rocked the baby, she could feel tears springing to her eyes—of pure joy, but also of a deep, longing regret. Ever since she was a girl, she'd envisioned having a family of her own: a husband who adored her, children who gazed up at her in wonder as she taught them everything she knew about the world. And the dirty diapers and the tantrums and the middle-of-the-night fevers, of course—she'd wanted it all. Desperately.

But duty had pulled her elsewhere, and by the time her mother had taken her last breath, Daphne looked around and realized that while she had been trying to save her mother's life, she'd lost a precious portion of her own.

Corinne was watching Daphne and Harper, her expression inscrutable, before she sighed heavily and pulled out a chair at the dining room table. She poured a glass of iced tea, grabbed Daphne's untouched plate of sandwiches, and pointed to the chair.

"Sit. Please."

She opened her arms for the baby, and Daphne pressed a soft kiss to the newborn's head before reluctantly passing her back to her mother. Corinne immediately called for the nanny—via a small brass bell on the table that Daphne found incredibly insulting—and when Harper had been carried away for a bottle and a nap, Daphne's sister turned her full attention to her.

"I need to talk to you." Corinne's blue eyes, so like Daphne's own, roamed over her face, and Daphne noticed that her sister had dropped the ridiculous upper-crust accent that she'd developed in the years since she'd married Raymond and become immersed in his high-society world.

"What's up?" She shifted uncomfortably in her chair as Corinne continued studying her and let out an uncomfortable laugh. "Do I have broccoli between my teeth or something?" Her fingers trailed along her lips, searching for the source of Corinne's scrutiny.

"No. Nothing like that." Corinne's perfectly manicured fingers were drumming frantically on the rim of her own glass, and her face was scrunched in thought. Finally, she sighed and said, "I want to talk about you."

"About me?" Daphne was taken aback. "What's wrong with me?" As she said those last words, the familiar insecurities began rearing their ugly heads.

No husband. No children. No education. No job.

Well, no *good* job at least.

"Nothing's wrong, per se. It's just that I'm worried about you. About the way your life has turned out so far." Corinne tucked a strand of blonde hair behind one ear, revealing a diamond stud that probably would have cost Daphne six months' worth of tips.

Daphne swallowed hard, her cheeks reddening. "I don't know what you're about to say, Corinne, but tread lightly. Just because you love living in a fancy home with your fancy husband doesn't mean that's the life for everyone. You know how much I love the island—I would never give it up. *Never.*" She squared off against her younger sister, the years of unspoken hurts and disappointments, the shadows of their broken childhood, hanging in the air between them. "I would never have given up on Mom."

"You think I gave up on her?" Corinne slapped the table, causing the crystal glasses to rattle. "She gave up on *herself*, Daph. No amount of telling yourself otherwise is going to change that. Dad left, and she fell apart. She didn't even bother taking care of us anymore. What was I, six years old when she started trying to find solace at the bottom of a bottle? She stopped being a mother to me when I was still practically a baby."

Corinne's cheeks were flushed as she clutched the edge of the dining table, knuckles white. "Never mind the fact that she never came to a single school function, or helped me with my homework, or God forbid asked me how my day was once in a while— she didn't even buy *food* for me, Daphne. You did that. With the money you earned at Sal's. You took care of everything for me, and for her, and you never took care of yourself."

"Yeah?" Daphne half-rose from the chair, her voice growing higher-pitched with anger. "And when you turned eighteen, what did you do? Did you stay and help me? Did you give me a break for a single second so I could do something that I wanted with my own life? Did you offer to pay for a single one of the bills, like the mortgage bill I was footing every month to keep the roof over your head? No." She practically spat the word. "You did nothing. You left, and you met Raymond, and you forgot we even existed."

"I did not." Tears of anger were welling in the corners of Corinne's eyes, but she didn't bother wiping them away. "I didn't forget about you. You're my sister, and I love you. But I couldn't *breathe*, Daphne. I couldn't breathe."

She pushed herself up from the table and began to pace the room in agitation. "I needed to get out of that house, and off that island, and away from the woman who couldn't pull herself together enough to care about us, or God forbid to love us. She ruined my childhood. Why should I have let her ruin the rest of my life too?"

She stopped pacing and stared hard at Daphne. "And I didn't abandon you. I begged you to come with me, or did you conveniently forget that part."

"I did not." Daphne met her sister's gaze with an equal amount of defiance. "But I wasn't going to leave our mother when she needed us the most."

"You mean like she did to us?" Corinne turned her face away and stared out the window. When she spoke again, her voice was broken. "Just because she was in that house every day doesn't mean she didn't leave us long ago. When she died, it was…"

She trailed off, her eyes on a young mother strolling past the window, holding a little boy's hand as they stopped to examine some flowers growing along the side of the road. Then she sighed heavily. "It was almost a relief."

She paused, waiting for Daphne to say something. When she didn't, Corinne said, so quietly Daphne had to strain to hear her, "It's not my fault that I fell in love with someone who could take care of me. It's not my fault I was able to get away."

She approached Daphne, grabbing her hand and holding on for dear life. "I've watched you, day after day, year after year, getting up each morning and doing the same thing. You're on a hamster wheel, and you don't seem to notice it. When Mom died, I thought you would finally spread your wings a little, maybe go to college or find a new job or even leave the island altogether, but… you didn't. Tell me, have you ever even let yourself fall in love? Let someone take care of *you* for once?"

Corinne took a deep breath, her gaze steady on Daphne's face. "Because every time I see you, Daphne, I'm afraid. I'm afraid that you're going to end up just like her—so unhappy that eventually you just… give up. And you deserve more than that. You deserve the world." She gave her a small, sad smile. "But you can't get the world if you don't allow yourself to take it."

CHAPTER 2

$\mathcal{J}$ana Martin inhaled deeply as the fresh aroma of coffee filled the inn's expansive kitchen, mingling with the tangy scent of newly painted walls and the saltwater air blowing in through the open window. It was another glorious day on the island, made even more special by the glorious evening that had preceded it.

Or maybe she should say the glorious evening, night, and early morning.

Time had felt like it was moving at warp speed as she and Reed sat on the beach for hours, sharing a bottle of champagne and a plate of Daphne's delectable desserts while they talked about anything and everything—from stories of their childhood to their hopes and dreams for the future. She could have spent endless days allowing his warm baritone laugh to drift over her skin as they huddled together to watch the sunrise, Reed's arm tucked around her waist as effortlessly as if it had been there her entire life and she'd only now just realized it.

When they had finally said goodbye with a soft, lingering kiss under an early-morning coral sky, Tana had practically floated up the steps to the inn's wraparound porch before collapsing into her favorite wicker chair and staring at the gently rippling water as she relived every second of it. Her reverie had been broken only by Luke Showalter, the contractor she'd chosen to head up the renovations to the inn, saying, with a Cheshire-cat grin, "Have a nice night?"

The best. It had been simply the best.

Tana felt silly now for the nerves that had overtaken her when she'd first seen Reed at the water's edge, bouquet of wildflowers in hand, gentle smile on his face as he showed her to the table he'd set up, complete with candles and romantic music. In that moment, she'd panicked—she'd convinced herself that she'd forgotten how to have an interesting conversation, or even how to kiss properly. But she was in her mid-forties with a grown daughter, for crying out loud—she'd lived an entire life before finding herself back on the island, and she'd managed to survive and even thrive.

Until. Until, until, until.

She hated that word.

She'd thrived *until* she found out her husband was carrying on with a much younger woman. She'd thrived *until* she found herself separated and selling the home they'd shared. She'd thrived *until* the dreams she'd always had for their future were shattered.

But now, that word was no more. She was thriving, plain and simple. Because she'd finally found a home. And more importantly, she'd finally found herself.

"Getting in a little late last night, hmm? You'd better hope I don't tell Mom—not that she'd care, of course."

Tana gave a start, and then, recognizing the voice speaking to her from the kitchen doorway, she swung around and stared at the man standing in front of her. Although it had been at least five years since she'd seen him, he still had the same sparkling blue-green eyes, thick, dark hair, and easy smile that held a hint of mischief around the edges.

"Jax!" Tana set down her mug of coffee with a

thunk and practically threw herself into her brother's arms. "What are you doing here?"

She pulled back to scrutinize his face. Up close, the lines around his eyes were more noticeable, and he looked... tired. Like a man drained of every last drop of energy.

"What's the matter?" she asked, her smile dropping. She led him to a chair at the counter and slid her mostly untouched coffee his way.

He gave her a grateful smile, then took a long sip, his eyes darting around the room. The kitchen was one of the few places in the inn that wasn't currently under construction, and it had become Tana's haven during the day, when the constant buzzing of saws and pounding of hammers began wearing away at her sanity.

"It's not like it used to be, is it?" Jax said, sidestepping her question. "I practically fell over from shock when I saw the old place—if this isn't a fall from grace, I don't know what is."

He shook his head, his brow furrowing. "When you told me over the phone that the inn needed repairs, I had no idea the extent of the problem. But this"—he waved his hand in a circular motion—"is a disaster. How could Uncle Henry have let this happen?"

Tana felt a surge of protectiveness for their great-uncle, a man who had spent most of his life building up walls to keep out the rest of the world, to prevent himself from making true connections and building friendships with others. He had recently righted the wrongs of his past, though, and Tana had high hopes that Henry would be able to live the rest of his life in peace and, dare she say, happiness.

In fact…

Tana checked her watch. Henry and Edie were due to begin their first date in less than an hour. Her stomach fluttered with nerves on her uncle's behalf —the man was over eighty years old and hadn't been on a date since he was a teenager. She couldn't imagine what was going through his mind right now, but she knew better than to knock on his bedroom door and check on him. Despite the strides he'd made, Henry still preferred his solitude. When he wanted to speak to Tana, he knew where to find her.

"It doesn't matter how he got here," Tana said, shaking her head. "What matters is that we're going to fix it. The renovations are going well… so well, in fact, that Luke, our contractor, thinks we'll be fully operational by the end of the summer." She sighed. "And then the real work begins."

"Well I'm here to help however I can," Jax said, crossing one leg over the other as he settled himself more comfortably in his chair. "I took some time off, and after hearing about everything you've been going through with the inn and Uncle Henry, I figured you could use an extra pair of hands." He waggled his fingers in the air and gave her a playful grin.

Instead of returning the smile, Tana gave her brother a suspicious look. "You took some time off? I can't remember the last time you had a true vacation from the restaurant—things there have always been too hectic for you to step away for more than a day or two."

She peered into his face, once more taking in the strain barely detectible beneath his smile. "Come on, Jax. I know you, remember? Just because we haven't seen each other in a while doesn't mean I can't tell when something's up." She leaned against the counter and crossed her arms over her chest. "Spill it."

Jax stared down into his coffee for several long moments, his brow furrowed as he traced his finger idly along the rim of the mug. Finally he looked up at her and sighed, his shoulders drooping, his body slumping further in his chair. "I lost it, Tana."

She gasped, hand flying to her mouth as she tried to process the news. He couldn't mean what she *thought* he did... could he?

"By 'it,' you mean..." She left the sentence unfinished, hoping if the words remained unspoken then they couldn't possibly be true.

Her brother nodded, eyes on his hands, which were now clenched in his lap. "All of it. The restaurant. My condo. My bank accounts. Everything."

Stunned, Tana pulled out the chair beside Jax and sank into it. She leaned forward and folded him into a long embrace. Then she sat back, wiping tears from her eyes, and whispered, "How could this be? The Brewhouse, it was so successful. Last I heard, you were running one of the hottest restaurants in Philadelphia."

Tana was still trying to wrap her head around what her brother was telling her. Jax had poured his heart and soul into that restaurant, had honed his talents as a chef for years at restaurants along the Eastern Seaboard until he'd finally settled in Philadelphia and realized his dream of opening up a place of his own. Within months, helped along by a series of fawning restaurant critic reviews that Tana had read with pride, The Brewhouse—and Jax, as the owner and head chef—was flying high. How had everything come crashing to the ground so quickly?

"I let my guard down." Jax's voice shook with anger as he clenched his hands into fists. "I was overworked, Tana… I was *so* overworked. You can't imagine what it's like, working nights and weekends and holidays, creating all the menus, overseeing the staff, handling the business end of things. My entire life was dedicated to the restaurant—I had no time for myself. I felt like I was going crazy sometimes."

He ran a hand through his dark hair, making it stand on end. "So I talked to one of my other buddies in the industry, and he recommended that I hire a business manager to take some of those things off my hands. But we were entering the holiday season, and we were overbooked with parties and events and just the regular evening crowds, and I was in such a rush to find someone, so desperate for help, that I hired someone without properly vetting them. She had a great resume, and stellar references, and a solid background—she seemed great."

There was something in his tone—a wistful note, maybe?—that Tana caught on to. She gave him a sharp look. "This woman. Were the two of you…?"

"Yes." Jax's jaw was set, his expression stone. "I thought she was the one. Her name was Genevieve, and she was gorgeous and funny and gregarious. And when she walked into a room, Tana, she set it on fire. Imagine how flattered I was when she decided I was worth her time."

His entire body was now slumped in defeat. "I let her take the reins of the restaurant's finances, and like an idiot, I never checked in on her. I believed everything she told me, until suddenly, little things weren't adding up. By the time the big things came to light and I realized that she was using the restaurant's profits to line her own pockets, she was gone. After that, I was never able to recover. I pumped my own money into the restaurant as much as possible, trying to overcome the damage, but it was too much. It was just too much."

He stared into his mug of coffee, glassy-eyed, as Tana watched him in horror. How had all of this been happening to her brother, right under her nose? Sure, they hadn't seen each other in several years—between her life on the West Coast and his busy schedule at the restaurant, they were rarely able to make time for in-person visits—but they still spoke on the phone semi-regularly.

Tana cast her mind back over those conversations, searching for anything he may have said, any hitch in his voice or tremor in his tone that would have signaled to her that something was off. But he was the same Jax as always—affable, teasing, easygoing. There was never any hint that underneath the surface, he was suffering.

"I'm so sorry," she said, blinking back tears of sadness and anger as she clutched her brother's hand and squeezed tightly. "I had no idea... if I had known, maybe Derek and I could have—"

"No." Jax shook his head emphatically, giving her a sharp look. "I would never have taken any handouts. I haven't done that at any point in my life, and I wouldn't have started now. You know I pride myself on being self-made, self-sufficient..." He trailed off, then let out a laugh devoid of any mirth. "I had no choice, did I? Julie made sure that we never really had anyone to rely on outside of ourselves."

Tana opened her mouth to argue, then quickly closed it again. Julie—which was what their mother preferred they call her—had been absent for large chunks of their life as children. She was a single mother who made her living as a wildlife photographer, often traveling to far-flung corners of the world while leaving her children with whatever relatives or friends she could cobble together on a moment's notice. Out of necessity, and a desire to let the past stay in the past, Tana had made peace with that aspect of her life years ago and now had a friendly if distant relationship with Julie. She'd always assumed Jax had felt the same way.

"Anyway." Jax took a long swig of coffee, then set his mug down hard on the counter. "Enough about our mother. When I found out what Genevieve had done, I filed police reports, talked to detectives, the whole enchilada. They've never been able to find her. The last detective who worked on the case didn't even think Genevieve was her real name. I had no choice but to close the restaurant, and I poured so much of my own money into it that I was so far behind on my mortgage that my condo was forced into foreclosure." He gave Tana a grim smile. "So when I told you I was taking some time off, what I really meant is that I have no other choice. I have no job, no house, no place to go, no—"

"No." Tana's voice was fierce as she stuck one finger under her brother's chin and forced him to meet her gaze. "You always, *always* have a place to go. You'll stay right here at the inn, with me and Uncle Henry." She swung her arm in an arc, indicating the ongoing construction. "Trust me, we'll find plenty of ways for you to help out. You can—"

"Cook!" Jax's eyes lit up as he glanced around the inn's kitchen. It now sat cold and empty, but in times past, when the inn had served breakfast to its guests, it had been a bustling place filled with delicious aromas and the infectious laughter of Bennet, the chef. When Tana had arrived on the island, she was devastated to learn that her uncle had been forced to let him go years ago. He had moved on, but the memories of him lingered in Tana's mind every time she stepped into the kitchen he'd loved so dearly.

But that was in the past. Right now, Tana had to focus on the present, and while she and Uncle Henry did plan on adding breakfast back to the inn's list of services, they only had the budget for a continental menu, and Tana had already enlisted Daphne's help. Her friend's homemade pastries were out of this world, and Tana knew that the opportunity meant the world to Daphne, who was counting on it as the catalyst that would help her leave her waitressing job at the diner once and for all.

But Jax was her brother, and the excitement in his eyes at the prospect of a new job, a new purpose, was a knife twisting in Tana's gut.

"I'm sorry," she said, wincing as his expression immediately sobered. "I've already promised the position to Daphne. Besides," she added in a hurry, hoping to soften the blow, "it's not a job for a chef with your level of experience. She's really just going to be providing pastries—you know, muffins, danishes, the occasional frittata. Nothing like what you're used to making."

She waved her hand airily as she continued. "Besides, why don't you take this as an opportunity to treat yourself to a little vacation? We could use your help around the inn here and there, but there's honestly not much to do right now. So rent a bike, spend time enjoying the beaches, read a good book."

The more animated she became, the more Jax perked up, until finally he said, "You're right. It's been a while since I've—"

"Jax, there you are."

Tana had been so busy trying to distract her brother that she hadn't heard the familiar thumping of Uncle Henry's cane until he was standing in the kitchen doorway. Although his date with Edie began in less than an hour, and despite the summer heat already seeping in through the windows, he was dressed in his usual uniform: a plaid flannel shirt, rumpled pants, and slippers. But Tana also caught a whiff of something in the air, something mildly spicy, something that smelled almost like…

"Is that cologne?" she asked, sidling up to her great-uncle and giving him a discreet sniff while he batted her away with his good hand.

"So what if it is?" he barked, his cheeks reddening. He thumped at her feet with his cane, his face scrunched in a scowl. "Now back off and stop smelling me. A man's got a right to a little privacy in his own house, doesn't he?"

"Sorry." Tana grinned at her uncle, and then, on impulse, leaned forward and kissed the old man's wrinkled cheek. "I'm just excited for you and Edie, that's all. I hope the two of you have a wonderful time. It's just..." She hesitated and glanced down at his slippers. "Don't you think you should put on a pair of real shoes?"

Henry followed her gaze to his feet, then frowned at her. "What do you think these are?"

Jax, who had been watching the exchange with amusement, chimed in, "I think you look great, Uncle Henry. I have no idea who Edie is or what the two of you are talking about, but you get a thumbs-up in my book."

He grinned at the two of them, and Tana shook her head and slipped back into her chair with a sigh. Henry was Edie's problem now, God bless her.

"Anyway." Henry shot Tana a dirty look, then turned his attention to Jax. "I just so happened to overhear part of your conversation, and I think it's a darn good idea."

"Sorry?" Jax cocked his head to one side and regarded the older man. "What's a good idea?"

"You. Here. The chef." Henry leaned against the counter as he waved his good hand around to indicate the kitchen. "You're family, and this is a family-run inn. Besides the fact that you're one of the best chefs on the East Coast, my father and grandfather would be turning over in their graves if they thought I wasn't helping out a family member in need. You need a job, we need someone to cook breakfast every morning. It's settled."

"But Uncle Henry." Tana stared at him in shock. "We've already promised that position to Daphne—and we were going with a continental menu, remember? We can't just go back on our word."

"And I don't want to step on anyone's toes." Jax held up his hands, palms out, and shook his head vigorously.

But the old man was undeterred. "Daphne's a good girl, and she'll understand. Besides, she has her job at the diner for now—she's not down on her luck like Jax. When we start to make more money, we'll bring her on, just as we planned to, and she can make all of her fancy muffins and donuts and what-have-yous. I've had a think about this, and I've decided that I want to serve a full breakfast like we used to. The guests liked it; I liked it. And I *am* still the owner, aren't I?"

He gave Tana a severe look. "We need a chef for that… and Daphne doesn't fulfill that requirement. So she's out, and Jax is in." He jabbed his cane at them, his eyes stern. "And that's final."

CHAPTER 3

*E*die Dawes straightened her turquoise shawl around her shoulders, patted her shoulder-length silver hair into place for what had to be the tenth time in the past two minutes, and flipped over the "open" sign on the door of Antiques on the Bay before turning her key in the lock. She wasn't normally in the habit of closing up the shop in the middle of the day during the height of tourist season, but today wasn't a normal day.

Today, she had a date. For the first time in over twenty years.

For the first time since her Johnny died.

A pang of guilt shot through her chest, but she did her best to quell it. She knew perfectly well that Johnny had wanted her to be happy; he'd told her so not long before the cancer had claimed his life. But "being happy" meant many different things, and in the years that had passed since she'd last seen his beautiful smile, didn't she cobble together a happy life?

She had moved to the serene island of Dolphin Bay and started a business of her own from scratch, had made friends and spent many mornings strolling along the beach, listening to the waves lapping against the shore and the gulls screeching overhead. She had found peace, and contentment, and serenity.

But had she found happiness?

She hadn't meant to fall in love again. She hadn't known a seventy-four-year-old widow with three grown children was even capable of falling in love again. But she had.

And now, her new beau was taking her out for lunch.

She just hoped he wasn't going to wear those darn slippers. And don't get her started on his old-man flannel shirts. So what if he actually *was* an old man? That didn't mean he couldn't be a snazzy dresser. Back in the day, her Johnny had worn a three-piece suit better than any man she'd ever seen, on screen or off. He made Clark Gable look like Mister Ed.

After one last glance at the shop door to make sure it was locked, Edie started off down the island's main street at a brisk pace, waving to her neighbors and fellow shopkeepers as she passed. That was one of the things she'd loved best about Dolphin Bay when she'd arrived, still freshly grieving and unsure what the rest of her life would bring. Everyone here was so friendly, so welcoming—they'd made her feel like one of their own, and before she knew it, she really was. Now she tried to do the same for other newcomers to the island, which was why she'd been so quick to befriend Tana, Henry's great-niece... and Reed's new girlfriend.

She was getting ahead of herself. They'd only been on one date. But Edie knew her son, and every time he looked at Tana, she saw in his eyes the same expression her Johnny had bestowed on her, every day of the week for the thirty-three years they were married.

Love.

Edie arrived at Sal's Diner and pushed open the door. She waved to Betty, one of the daytime hostesses, before making a beeline for her and Henry's favorite table by the window, where they'd agreed to meet. Henry had wanted to pick her up in his golf cart, but she'd declined—she'd needed to walk off some of her nervous energy before the date started. He'd also wanted to take her to one of those fancy restaurants on the mainland, but Edie had declined that too. She wanted their first date to be here, at the very place where they started to fall in love.

Only this time, they were going to make it official.

When she arrived at the table, Edie's breath caught in her throat. She couldn't count the number of times they'd shared a meal here, but never before had the table been set with a white cloth, or adorned with candles and several bouquets of stunning red roses. And standing beside her side of the booth, leaning heavily on his cane and smiling nervously, was Henry.

"Hi." He raised his hand in an awkward greeting, half-wave, half-salute.

Edie sighed. Only Henry. And was he…?

Yes. She peered at his slipper-clad feet. He was.

And she couldn't possibly have cared less.

"You old kook," she said, taking a step forward and gently cupping his cheek. "What did you go to all this trouble for? It's only me."

"Yeah, well, that's the point, isn't it?" Henry met

her gaze, his green eyes piercing. "It's you." Then he held out his hand, and she took it, allowing him to guide her into her seat—with a lot of maneuvering of his cane and grunts that she tactfully ignored.

"Sorry," he said, scowling in frustration as he lowered himself into his own seat, using his good hand to brace himself. "I'm not as agile as I used to be."

"Henry Turner, I've known you for twenty years, and never would I ever use the word 'agile' to describe you, before the stroke or after." Edie's tone was gently teasing, and after a moment, Henry shrugged and grinned at her.

"No, I suppose not. But a man wants to make a good impression when he takes his sweetheart out for a date, doesn't he?" His face was almost purple with embarrassment, and Edie felt a rush of affection as she reached across the table and rested her hand on his arm.

"You make a wonderful impression just by being you." She picked up her menu, then slid one across the table toward him. "Now stop being so formal and order me some French fries."

Two hours later, Henry stood behind Edie as she fished in her purse for her key and unlocked the door to her shop. "Thank you for a wonderful time," she said, pushing open the door and then turning to face him. "I can't remember when I last had such a lovely lunch."

And she couldn't. Despite their slightly awkward start, Henry had been the perfect gentleman—attentive, conversational, complimentary. As the lunch progressed, he'd gradually come out of his shell, and Edie had been thrilled to discover that underneath his slightly gruff exterior, Henry was an affectionate, warm man. After the main course, during which the conversation flowed easily and their laughter filled the diner, causing more than one head to turn their way, they'd shared a slice of cheesecake for dessert—and Edie had even joined him on his side of the booth, resting her head on his shoulder as he gently stroked her hand.

"I had a wonderful time too, Edie."

Henry stepped closer to her, stabilizing himself against the side of the building so he could use his good hand to cup her cheek. She closed her eyes against his touch, knowing that this moment—this goodbye—would be the thing to change their relationship forever. They'd been more than friends for many years, but neither had acknowledged their feelings—their true feelings—out loud.

She heard him take a deep breath, and then there was a moment of hesitation before soft lips were pressed against hers in a kiss that was tender and full of longing, a culmination of the unspoken feelings that had lingered between them for far too long. She wrapped her arms around his neck and gave herself fully to the moment, and when they finally broke apart, Edie opened her eyes to find him staring down at her with an intense gaze.

"I'm eighty-three years old, Edie, and I don't know how much more time I have left on this earth." Henry reached out his good hand and stroked her chin, his eyes never leaving her face. "I know this might seem like it's too early to say, but it's also been nearly twenty years in the making." He inhaled sharply, then let his breath out with a whoosh. "I love you."

Edie stepped forward and allowed herself to be wrapped in his one-armed embrace. She was vaguely aware of passersby on the street stepping around them, some whispering and glancing their way with smiles, but she was too lost in the moment to care. She squeezed him gently, then pulled away from him and caressed his wrinkled cheek while he closed his eyes against the touch of her fingers.

"I love you too, Henry."

She felt a pang as Johnny's face filled her mind. Edie had never said those words to another man in her life—outside of her son, of course. Hearing them come out of her lips now seemed like a betrayal, a final acknowledgement that she and Johnny would never again meet in this lifetime. But it also awakened in her a sense of hope and happiness that she'd long suppressed, a feeling that she could still reach out and grab what she wanted out of life.

And it was this. She wanted this.

"I want you to know that my intentions are sincere," Henry said, opening his eyes and meeting her gaze once more. "I don't have time to play around. You and I—we're not spring chickens anymore, Edie. We're..." He pursed his lips, searching for the right word. "We're old ducks."

"Old *ducks*?" Edie shook her head. "You always were a flatterer, Henry. You really know how to make a girl feel good about herself." She placed her hands on her hips as a smile played across her lips. "I'll forgive you for that last comment if you kiss me again."

And so he did.

CHAPTER 4

*T*ana stared down at the paper in her trembling hands. It must have arrived yesterday, though she'd only noticed it poking out of the mailbox when she'd returned from her early morning stroll along the beach. She'd been expecting it—in fact, she was the one who'd requested it.

But that didn't make seeing it in person any easier.

"You okay, sis?" Jax sidled up beside her and peered down at the letter. "This is what you wanted, right?"

"It is." Tana sighed as she folded the paper and slipped it back into the envelope. "But at the same time, it's not, you know? Derek and I are officially separated. By law." She leaned against the inn's front desk and gazed out the picture window, which over-looked the beach and the island's beautiful red-and-white lighthouse.

"Do you remember our wedding? I spent the whole day pinching myself—I couldn't believe how lucky I was to have found a man like him. When I think back to that girl, I can't imagine how she would have felt, knowing things would end up like they did."

She shook her head sadly. "I wanted this separation, but I also wish it never had to happen in the first place. The memories I have of our time together —and so many of them are good—will forever be tainted by what he's done."

She bent the envelope absentmindedly between her fingers. "I just wish California didn't require a six-month waiting period before the divorce. I'd rather make a clean, quick break, move on with my life. Right now, I feel like I'm in arrested development."

"You aren't, though." Jax slung an arm around her shoulder and squeezed. "Look at all the amazing things you have going on in your life—like helping Uncle Henry restore the inn, for one. I really think it's given you a new purpose."

"It has," Tana acknowledged. "After Emery left for

college, I could never quite figure out what to do with my days. There are only so many luncheons I can attend before wanting to tear my hair out." She laughed—the days she spent with the other wives of Hollywood bigwigs seemed like an eternity ago. "I'm really, truly happy here—but I'm sad too, if that makes sense."

"It makes perfect sense. You're mourning your old life and celebrating the new happiness you've found because of it." Jax nudged her in the arm. "From what I've gathered, some of that happiness might be attributed to a certain new man in your life?"

Tana felt a sudden lightness in her heart as she pictured Reed's face. "He's wonderful," she said, smiling softly. "The kind of man a woman could fall head over heels for. I'm just afraid..." She trailed off, and Jax gave her a knowing look.

"You're afraid history's going to repeat itself," he supplied. A look of anger flashed across her brother's face. "I always liked Derek, but right now, I'll be honest—if he stepped foot in this inn today, I'd have no qualms about punching him squarely in the nose."

Tana laughed. "And what would that get you other than a night in jail? Not that I haven't imagined doing the same thing about a thousand times over, of course. But honestly, he's not worth the time or effort it would take to do that. I hate what he did to me, and to our family, but I'm not going to be a victim any longer."

An idea struck her, and she unfolded the separation agreement and placed it on a prominent spot on the front desk. "Now I can look at it every day to remind myself not to live in the past, but to embrace the future." She checked the time on her phone. "And speaking of which, I'm about to surprise Reed at his job with a little picnic on the beach. Would you like to come with me? I'm dying for the two of you to meet—I know you're going to love him."

Jax smirked. "As romantic as that sounds, I think I'm going to take a few hours and jot down some sample ideas for the inn's breakfast menu." He hesitated, his face darkening. "About that... I have to say, I'm really uncomfortable with this whole thing, but Uncle Henry is insistent. Have you spoken to Daphne yet?"

"No." Tana winced. "I know I have to... but yesterday, she was planning to visit her sister and meet her new baby niece, and I didn't want to spoil her day with bad news. I'm still hoping that Uncle Henry will change his mind—I know he means well, and as the inn's owner, the decision is entirely up to him, but his logic about Daphne already having a job isn't going to go over well with her. She's miserable at the diner, and she's been viewing this as her ticket to a new career."

She massaged her forehead, which had begun throbbing. "I don't even know what I'm going to say to her."

"Great," Jax muttered. "Just great. Maybe I should tell Uncle Henry that I can't take the job? When I made the suggestion to you, I wasn't really thinking through the implications of what I was saying. I have no intentions of staying on the island long-term—I just need a place to regroup and make a plan for the future, figure out what I'm going to do with the rest of my life." He laughed hollowly.

Tana heaved a sigh. "The problem now is that Uncle Henry is dead-set on having a full breakfast, and he's right—Daphne isn't a chef. Our contractor Luke thinks the inn will be up and running fairly soon, so why don't you just stay on during the grand reopening and while we iron out the kinks, and then you can train someone else to be your replacement? Hey!"

Her face brightened, and she smacked a palm to her forehead. "You can train Daphne! I don't know why I didn't think of this earlier. I'm sure she'd love to take the job. I'll call her right now."

Tana reached for her phone, but Jax stopped her with a hand on her arm. "No. Don't call Daphne. Please." His voice held an edge of panic that caused Tana to stare at him in concern.

"Okay," she said slowly, then frowned at him. "What's the problem?"

"I just…" Jax raked both hands through his dark hair and blew out a breath. "This is all happening a little too quickly, okay? My life's been a nightmare these past couple of years, and I only stepped foot on the island two days ago, and somehow I already have a new job that I'll be leaving in a few months, along with the responsibility of training someone to take over for me in a position I've never even held. I need a breather."

"It's okay." Tana rested a hand on his arm and gave it a gentle squeeze. "Trust me, I understand. Why don't you take a few hours and go down to the beach? It's a beautiful day, and I don't know about you, but the fresh sea air always does wonders for me when I need a chance to clear my head."

She reached behind the front desk and held up the picnic basket she'd packed earlier. "As a matter of fact, I'll be doing the exact same thing."

∾

TANA WAS STILL REFLECTING on her conversation with her brother as she walked along the beach toward the hut where Reed operated Dolphin Bay Adventures, the water sports rental and island tour company he had built from the ground up. She hoisted the picnic basket over to her other arm, regretting that she'd gone just a tad overboard when deciding what to bring for their picnic—in hindsight, they definitely hadn't needed the scented candles, and they probably could have skipped out on the giant jug of homemade lemonade she'd prepared, too.

But Tana hadn't planned a date in ages—she and Derek had been well past the point in their marriage where they surprised each other with romantic gestures like picnics; which, she supposed, said a lot about the state of their relationship.

As she approached the hut, she squinted inside but couldn't see Reed, only a trio of teenage boys selecting from a lineup of surfboards mounted to the back wall, helped by a redheaded woman Tana didn't recognize but she assumed to be Kelly, Reed's assistant. When the woman thanked the boys and they trooped away, surfboards tucked under their arms, Tana caught a glimpse of her face and felt her heart sink into her stomach.

The woman was gorgeous—tall and slender, with huge brown eyes framed by dark lashes and cheekbones that could cut glass. She could easily give Lucia, Derek's mistress, a run for her money in the looks department. And to add insult to injury, she was wearing a bikini top that showcased her cobbled abs and generous cleavage.

Tana glanced down at her plain tank top and loose khaki shorts and winced, then forced a smile onto her face and approached the woman, who was busy counting the money in the cash register.

"Hi," she said uncertainly, waiting for the woman to look up from her task. When she did, she gave Tana a pleasant smile that revealed—of course—a dimple in each cheek.

"Welcome to Dolphin Bay Adventures. I'm Kelly. How can I help you?"

"I'm looking for Reed Dawes." Tana held up the picnic basket, and Kelly eyed it for a long moment. Then her gaze swept up and down Tana's body in a way that made her feel distinctly uncomfortable. "Can you please let him know Tana is here?"

"Last name?" the woman asked, her voice suddenly sharp.

"Martin." Tana frowned at her. "But he knows who I am."

Kelly produced a pad of paper and a pen, then jotted down Tana's name. "He isn't here right now, but I'll be sure to let him know you were looking for him." She gave Tana a sugary-sweet smile. "If you'd like, I can give him a call on his *personal* cell." The way she said the word implied a familiarity that set Tana's teeth on edge—who was this woman, anyway?

"No thanks," she bit out. "I don't want to bother him. I'll just—"

"Tana!"

She turned to find Reed striding up the beach, kicking up sand in big clumps as he walked. His skin was dewy from the ocean, and his sunglasses were pushed on top of his dark hair. Trailing behind him was a group of men and women who looked both exhausted and exhilarated—his latest kayak group tour, no doubt.

He turned to the group as they approached the hut, thanking them for their business and delivering handshakes all around, and then jogged over to Tana's side.

"Hey," he said, sweeping her into his arms and holding on tight. She allowed herself to sink into him, noticing from the corner of her eye that Kelly was watching them with a sour expression. Reed pulled back and eyed the picnic basket. "What's all this?"

"I thought it might be nice to have a little afternoon date." Tana patted the basket and smiled shyly at him. "If you're up for it, of course. Can you sneak away for thirty minutes?"

She lifted the top of the basket and waved her hand over it, wafting imaginary food smells in Reed's direction. "I pulled out all the stops—I may even have snuck over to Sal's Diner and snagged a couple portions of the cherry crisp with vanilla ice cream that I know you love so much."

Reed groaned and pressed a hand to his stomach. "What are you trying to do to me, woman?" He lightly kissed her temple. "I think I have some time— let me ask Kelly to check the schedule just to be sure. These summer days are usually booked solid, but it was overcast this morning, and the clouds scared away some of the people who otherwise would have booked a tour."

He made a beeline for the hut, where Kelly was busy returning the kayakers' personal items they hadn't wanted to risk getting wet, and waited until the last person had trooped away. Then he leaned through the window to speak to her, gesturing to something on the desk. Kelly frowned at him before cutting her eyes to Tana, then shook her head at Reed and said something that Tana couldn't hear. Reed's response came with raised eyebrows, but then he turned and shot Tana a quick thumbs-up.

She grinned at him, and then busied herself unpacking the picnic things. She was just peeling the lid off a plastic container of cubed watermelon when he jogged back over to her. "I'm all yours for the next forty-five minutes," he whispered in her ear, holding her close for a few moments before releasing her to help her unpack.

He grabbed a striped tablecloth from the basket and unfolded it, laying it down in the sand before rummaging around for the candles, matches, and silverware. "Wow, you didn't miss anything," he said with a laugh as he lit the candles and set them carefully in the sand. "If you asked me to pack a picnic, you would have been lucky if I remembered something to drink. Or eat, for that matter."

"Remember, I'm a mom," Tana said in a teasing tone. "I had years of practice packing anything a growing girl needed in my purse. And if I thought things were hairy when Emery was a baby, that was *nothing* compared to what it was like when she became a teenager." She shuddered playfully, then gave the basket a shake for good measure. "I'm an expert by now. If this were an Olympic sport, I would win the gold medal every time."

As she crouched down to lay out their plates, Tana glanced at the hut—and once again, Kelly was watching them, arms folded across her chest. She gave Tana a quick, tight smile when she caught her eye, and then grabbed an armful of towels, exited the hut, and busied herself with wiping down the kayaks in preparation for the next tour. Every so often, though, she snuck a glance in their direction—and was it Tana's imagination, or was Kelly purposely bending down far enough to flaunt her cleavage and miniscule jean shorts? She once more tugged at her own shirt, noticing with a slightly sick feeling that a group of men stood nearby, openly ogling Reed's assistant.

"Yoo-hoo. Earth to Tana?"

Reed was watching her with an amused expression, which quickly faded to one of discomfort when he followed Tana's gaze to Kelly and the men.

"Sorry," she said with a wince. "I shouldn't even be saying this to you, because it makes me feel far worse, but I can't help but notice something… off… about your assistant. Do you two…"

She trailed off, wondering whether she was out of place for voicing her concerns. After all, she and Reed had only gone on one official date.

"Do we have a history?" Reed said gently. He took Tana's hand, his pale blue eyes roving over her face, his expression serious. "No. Kelly's a flirt, and she's made it clear to me over the past few months that she'd be up for something more than a business relationship, but I have zero interest."

He gave her hand a squeeze, his thumb stroking her palm. "I told you I wanted to see where this led, Tana, and I meant it. When I'm in a relationship with someone, I don't stray. I'm not Derek, and I won't ever become him. It's not how I operate."

Tana flinched at his last words, because there was a time not so long ago when she never would have thought Derek was capable of being anything other than a wonderful, attentive husband. Now he was on the wrong end of an unflattering comparison.

She considered Reed's words for a moment, her eyes lingering on Kelly, and then she nodded. "Okay. And sorry again—I used to have a lot of self-confidence, but what I've gone through has eaten away at most of it. I want to trust you, and I do—I just… it's going to take time."

"That's okay with me." Reed gave her hand one

last squeeze before releasing it and grinning at her. "I'm a patient man—I've got all the time in the world." He checked his watch. "Thirty-eight minutes, to be exact."

Tana gave him a playful slap on the shoulder, then deliberately turned away from Kelly and the gawking men. She was being ridiculous—Reed was decidedly *not* Derek, and she wasn't going to put the brakes on a new, exciting, and promising relationship just because her insecurities were rearing their ugly heads. Besides, if there was one thing she had learned throughout the past few weeks, it was that she needed to take a step back and live in the moment. And right now, she was on a date with a warm, wonderful, caring man.

"Cheers," Reed said, raising his sandwich in the air and bumping it against Tana's glass of lemonade. "And now, let's enjoy this beautiful day together."

Tana leaned back, tipped her head to the sky, and smiled, intent on doing just that.

CHAPTER 5

*D*aphne exhaled heavily as she stepped outside the grease-stained diner air and into the fresh, ocean-tinged breeze. She ripped her apron off and stuffed it inside her oversized purse, then cast one last glance over her shoulder at the diner's packed interior before hurrying down the island's main drag. The afternoon shift had been endless, and the tips scrawny—as was usually the case when Sal's was overtaken by tourists, pushing out the regulars. How someone could justify spending thousands on a vacation and then leave a two-dollar tip on a hundred-dollar tab was unfathomable to Daphne, and more than a little disheartening.

Worse, she was still reeling from the conversation she'd had with her sister the day before, and all throughout the sleepless night Daphne had endured after returning to her apartment on the island, Corinne's words were echoing in her mind.

Every time I see you, Daphne, I'm afraid. I'm afraid that you're going to end up just like her—so unhappy that eventually you just... give up.

More arguing had followed that proclamation, and at one point it got so heated that the baby woke up and began crying. Daphne had left not long after that, taking whatever scraps of dignity she had left with her. It would be a long, long time before she ventured back into Corinne's picture-perfect life again. She didn't want to cramp her style.

Or hear that her sister thought she was living a miserable life. Which was patently untrue.

Right?

Right, Daphne thought fiercely, clenching her hands into fists at her sides as the inn came into view. Several men were working on the roof, shouting instructions to each other as they replaced missing shingles and patched up the bent gutters. A warm feeling came over Daphne as she watched them, knowing that in a few short weeks, the inn would be up and running, a phoenix rising from the ashes to soar once more.

And she would rise right along with it.

Until Daphne had boarded the ferry for the return trip to the island, able to breathe again following the stifling air in her sister's massive home, she didn't realize quite how much pressure she was putting on her new job at the inn—she would only be supplying breakfast treats to the guests, and if that went well, goodies for in-room baskets would be added at some point in the future. She certainly wouldn't be making enough money to leave her job at the diner, but still, the opportunity felt like a springboard to her future. A way for her to finally shed the job that had been weighing her down for twenty-five years and allow herself to envision a new kind of life, one where she was waking up each morning with a smile on her face, knowing that she was doing something she loved.

Reed was a perfect example of what life could be like. He had turned his passion for water sports into a growing, thriving business that was more successful with each passing year. He loved his job— Daphne could see the light in his eyes every time he talked about it, even when he was complaining about a difficult day or broken equipment. He could take the good with the bad because at the end of the day, he was happy.

Was Daphne happy?

Right now, that question was just... too much. What she needed was a friend, someone who could give her a reality check, someone who could reassure her that everything was going to be okay. What she needed was Tana.

As she approached the inn, she could see the back of Tana's favorite wicker chair on the porch rocking slowly as her friend enjoyed the picturesque ocean view. Even though the day had started off cloudy—which had caused the tourists to flock to the diner to wait out the anticipated rain over coffee and pancakes—the sky was now a brilliant blue, so clear that the dark shapes of trees on the mainland were visible at this distance. The sand below the inn was dotted with colorful umbrellas, and the sounds of children laughing and playing in the waves floated over to her as she bounded up the cobblestone sidewalk before taking the steps two at a time.

Daphne crossed the porch and reached over to tap her friend on the shoulder—Tana had an earbud in each ear, presumably listening to music—and then she stopped short. Unless Tana's hair had grown several shades darker and she'd chopped it off to above her ears, someone else had taken over her friend's favorite chair. Maybe a member of the construction crew?

And then the chair's occupant turned around, causing Daphne's breath to catch and her throat to constrict in panic.

Not Tana. Or anyone else she wanted to see, now or ever again.

"Hey."

Jax Keller bolted upright at the sight of Daphne's face, which she was certain had lost all color. He fumbled with the phone in his lap, then tugged out his earbuds and stuffed them into his pocket. Then he stood to greet her, and as his blue-green eyes latched onto hers, she felt like all of the air had been sucked out of the atmosphere; the roar of the ocean and the playful screams of the children faded into the background, until the only sound Daphne could hear was her own shallow breathing.

"What are *you* doing here?" she demanded when she could finally speak again.

Jax visibly recoiled at the fire in her voice, then shoved his hands into the pockets of his jeans and offered her a weak smile. "Don't sound so happy to see me." He hesitated, then took a step toward her and held out his arms. "It's good to see you, Daph. What's it been, twenty-five years?"

"No." Daphne swatted his arm away. "You do not get to touch me, Jax. Not anymore." Her voice caught unexpectedly on the last word, and she cleared her throat to cover the awkward moment. Folding her arms tightly over her chest, she added, "You lost that right a long time ago."

"Yeah. Sure. Of course." Jax blew out a breath. "Sorry."

For what?

The question lingered in the air between them as Daphne forced herself to stare into those eyes, the ones she'd gotten lost in every summer for ten years. They had always reminded her of the ocean on a clear day, and they caused memories she had long buried to come tumbling to the surface: their first kiss, shared as they were tucked into one of the island's secluded coves, the moonlight shining down on them like a lover's caress; their first date, when they'd stayed at Sal's Diner half the night, giggling over chocolate malts and dancing to the tunes on the jukebox; their first fight, which was over something silly that Daphne couldn't even remember, but she did remember the way he'd held her afterward, as though he never wanted to let her go.

There hadn't been a last fight. There'd been nothing but radio silence for twenty-five years. And that indifference had hurt her far worse than any angry words they could have thrown at each other.

She couldn't do this. Not now, not tomorrow, not in ten years or twenty or thirty. She had packed him away in the furthest corners of her mind more than two decades ago, and she had no intentions of allowing him to roam free again, to open up the raw wounds she'd so carefully bandaged over before moving on with her life.

"Is Tana here?"

Daphne made a show of glancing over Jax's shoulder in search of her friend, but she could see through the inn's picture window that the front desk was empty. Jax shook his head in confirmation, his hands still shoved deep in his pockets, his face screwed up in a half-smile, half-wince that actually looked painful. Beads of sweat were sprouting on his forehead, but he made no move to swipe them away.

"She's on a date, with someone named Reed?" Jax finally slid his hands out of his pockets and raked his fingers through his hair until it was standing on end, a nervous habit he'd had since he was a teenager. "I don't know when she'll be back... but if you're interested, we could have a glass of iced tea, maybe catch up a little?"

He waved his hand toward the pair of wicker chairs usually occupied by Daphne and Tana. "You know, if you have time," he added after an awkward extended silence.

Daphne continued staring at him, speechless, unsure whether she wanted to laugh at the absurdity of his suggestion or slap him across the face.

Catch up a little? Sure, Jax, let's catch up. Why don't you go ahead and tell me why you stopped answering my letters and phone calls out of the blue. Or why you never showed up on the island for the visit you promised to make, the one where I was positive we were going to get engaged, like we always talked about? Or why you broke every single promise you ever made to me?

She almost sat down then. She almost sat down, and crossed her legs, and made herself comfortable, and demanded to know why he'd let her think he would save her when he'd been the one to shatter her to pieces. If the demise of their relationship had happened now, she could have handled it. But back then, she was just a kid, working her fingers to the bone at the diner during the day so she could pay the bills and keep a roof over her and her sister's heads while spending her evenings trying to hide her mother's ever-growing collection of alcohol bottles, most of which would be empty by the time the sun rose in the coral-streaked morning sky. Or trying to shield Corinne from the sound of their mother's crying, which always lasted deep into the night, when she thought the darkness would conceal her from the daughters she'd abandoned in almost every way long ago.

Stupid, really, if she thought about it. No one had ever taken care of Daphne; she'd had to rely on herself for almost as long as she could remember. Why had she expected Jax to be any less of a disappointment than everyone else around her?

And now he wanted to have iced *tea* with her?

"No," she said coolly, hitching her purse over her shoulder. "And no need to tell Tana I stopped by—I'll catch up with her some other time." Then she swung on her heel and walked down the porch steps and along the inn's cobblestone sidewalk until she was out of sight.

Only then did she begin to run.

~

JAX WATCHED HER WALK AWAY, surprised that his hands were trembling slightly. Maybe she still had an effect on him after all these years. Maybe it was the guilt.

He stared after her long after she had disappeared, then turned and quietly padded into the inn. Ignoring Uncle Henry at the front desk and the men plodding through the hallways, lugging building equipment and erecting scaffolding, he made a beeline for the kitchen.

For the kitchen cabinet over the sink, to be more exact.

For what was *inside* that cabinet, if he wanted to get really technical about it.

His first day at the inn, he'd walked into the kitchen to find his sister on her tiptoes, reaching into that very cabinet, pulling out a bottle of wine that glistened with promise. And danger.

Always danger.

"Do you want some?" she'd asked innocently, completely unaware of the tornado those four simple words had unleashed inside him. He couldn't remember the last time someone had offered him a drink.

He'd served alcohol at The Brewhouse; there'd been no choice, if he wanted a successful gastropub that would cater to the younger crowd. But his bartender, Shayna, had been one of the few people he'd confided in, and she knew that Jax's visits to the bar to check in on her would be infrequent. When she needed something, she could always find him in the kitchen—his home, his sanctuary.

He didn't crave it—not anymore. But it was always lingering on the periphery of his senses, a seductive promise, a way to forget. It had almost ruined his life. In many ways—and in the most important way of all—it had ruined it, opening up a void that had threatened to drown him. Years of intense therapy had allowed him to finally, finally claw to the surface, to find his way back into the light.

But right now, after everything he had gone through—losing his restaurant, his home, his future —that bottle of wine, innocent to most people, was a siren beckoning him into a swirling sea.

Unlike Tana, Jax was tall enough to reach above the sink with no trouble. He lifted his arm now, as if on autopilot, and winced as the aging cabinet door creaked open, the sound like a gunshot in the silent kitchen. His fingers caressed the smooth glass, and after a single breath of hesitation, he lifted it down from its perch and held it in one hand. He gazed at the bottle as the seconds ticked into minutes, until he finally uncorked it, the satisfying *pop* echoing throughout the empty space.

And then, with a deep inhale and a feeling of strength blackened by only a hint of regret, he exhaled, long and loud, before dumping the entire bottle down the drain.

CHAPTER 6

*E*die hummed as she swept the shop floor, which she prided herself on keeping as immaculate as it had been on the day she'd moved in. After the soaring success of their lunch date, she and Henry had met for dinner that same night, and breakfast the following morning. Their progression from friendship to something deeper had become, to Edie, as natural as breathing.

She wasn't experiencing the swept-off-her-feet, stars-in-her-eyes feelings she'd been struck with the first time she'd met her Johnny. This was a quieter romance—less fire and passion, more warmth, comfort, and gentleness. But it was no less exciting, and in many ways, even more so, because it had come at an unexpected time in her life, when she believed that her heart had been closed off in that way for good.

It had been, and continued to be, a wonderful surprise, and she was determined to make the most of every moment of it. And this evening, she was excited to share the news with two of the most important people in her world.

The bell above the shop door chimed and the sound of laughter followed, and Edie set aside her broom and dustpan and turned to greet her daughters with open arms. Laurie and Karina both lived only a quick ferry ride away on the mainland, but their busy schedules with work and children kept them from visiting as often as Edie would have liked. She had known that would come with the territory when she decided to move to Dolphin Bay, but she missed their daily presence in her life all the same.

"My girls!" she said, greeting them as she had since they still wore pigtails and collared dresses. She pulled each of them into a hug, holding on tightly before stepping back to look them over with a motherly eye. Both looked happy, and healthy, and vibrant, which was everything she could have asked for.

"The shop looks great, Mom," Laurie, her eldest,

said as she glanced around at the stocked shelves and rows of antique furniture. "How's business?"

"Good as ever," Edie said proudly as she unhooked her shawl from the coat rack and slipped it over her shoulders. "The summer season is in full swing, which means I barely have a second to sneak away for lunch. You know I wouldn't have it any other way, though."

"But you're taking care of yourself, right?" Karina chimed in, sweeping her eyes over her mother's face in concern. "Reed tells us you're at the shop morning till night. Don't you think that's a bit much at your age?"

"At what age?" Edie said in mock irritation, pressing her hands to her hips. "And besides, I can rest when I'm dead."

She was parroting back the familiar phrase her own mother had so often used, and as Edie grew older, she began to realize the wisdom behind the words. Keeping active was an essential part of her well-being, and she planned to operate Antiques on the Bay for as long as she could.

"We just worry about you, that's all," Laurie said, slinging an arm over her mother's shoulders. "Kind of like you worried about us for all those years?"

She turned to her sister with a grin. "Do you

remember when we were teenagers and you brought home that guy… what was his name?" She pursed her lips in thought, then snapped her fingers. "Bobby Delgado. He had tattoos from here to here"—she swept her fingers from wrist to shoulder—"he drove a motorcycle, and he even had a pierced ear. When he came roaring into the driveway on that bike, I thought Mom was going to have a heart attack."

"I forgot about him," Karina said, her voice filled with laughter. "Mom and Dad made me promise to never get on the back of that bike, so I always made sure he dropped me off a full block from home so they wouldn't see me climbing down. I hate to admit it, though, but our parents were right—he was a troublemaker. But we had a lot of fun that summer," she added, glancing into the distance with a smile.

"I have news for you," Edie said, shaking her head as she followed her daughters to the shop door, flipping off the lights before opening it and stepping out onto the sidewalk. "Your father and I knew perfectly well what you were doing—and we also knew a boy like that wouldn't last. But if we had put too many restrictions on you, we only would have pushed you further in his direction. If I recall," she added with a sly smile, "the end of that same summer is when you met Gavin."

Karina grinned at the mention of her husband. "And look at me now—no motorcycles in sight. But if I'm ever feeling dangerous, I can always have him rev up the minivan."

The three women headed down the sidewalk, the ocean breeze tousling their hair and the waning sun playing softly across their faces. Many of Edie's fellow shopkeepers were closing for the evening, and the number of tourists strolling along the island's main drag was dwindling as they headed for dinner and their hotels. In the distance, the ferry glided toward the island, and the cry of a single gull circling overhead followed them as they walked.

"I love coming here," Laurie said with a sigh as she gazed out over the gently rippling water. "You couldn't have chosen a more perfect place to live, Mom. Sometimes I'm sorry Owen and I didn't move here when we had the chance. Our lives are so hectic on the mainland... sometimes I crave a slower pace."

Karina nodded her agreement as the three women approached the door to Sal's Diner. Before they could reach for the handle, the door swung open, and Reed and Tana strolled out, hand in hand.

"Hey!" he said in surprise when he saw his sisters. He released Tana's hand to give each woman a kiss on the cheek. "I didn't know you were coming to the island today. I would have joined you for dinner, but Tana and I stopped in for an early bite."

He turned to Tana, a soft smile playing across his lips. "I'd like to introduce you to my sisters, Karina and Laurie. My *older* sisters," he added, eyes twinkling.

The women made noises of protest, then greeted Tana with hugs while Edie stood back, her heart swelling with happiness as she took in the scene. Her own parents had always emphasized the importance of family, a lesson she and Johnny had worked hard to instill in their children. Too many siblings went their separate ways as the years passed and they began to build families of their own, and she was proud that her children had managed to maintain a close bond into adulthood.

She also couldn't help but note the way Reed kept his arm wrapped around Tana's waist, how they leaned into each other as they laughed and chatted with her daughters. She had no doubt that her son was falling hard for Henry's niece, and from the softness in Tana's gaze every time she looked Reed's way, she could tell that Tana felt the same way. Edie had watched anxiously from the sidelines for years as Reed half-heartedly dated a string of women, none of whom were ever right for him, and she sincerely hoped that this time he had struck gold.

A few moments later, Reed and Tana said goodbye and began walking down the street, arms linked, her head resting on his shoulder. Laurie sighed wistfully as she watched them leave. "Don't get me wrong, I love being married—but there's something magical about a new relationship. Tana seems really nice. I hope things work out for them."

"She's a wonderful girl," Edie confirmed as they entered the diner and greeted Betty, the same hostess who had been working during her first date with Henry. As she slid three menus off the pile and gestured for them to follow her to an empty booth in the corner, she gave Edie a knowing smile.

"I expected to see you here with your new gentleman friend. A little birdie on the staff tells me that the two of you have had no less than three dates here at the diner over the past two days."

Although Betty was trying to keep her voice low, Edie noticed her daughters' ears perking up. They exchanged questioning glances, but waited until they were settled in their booth with glasses of water before barraging their mother with questions.

"A date? We didn't know you had one date, let alone three. And all in the past two *days*?"

"What exactly is a 'gentleman friend?' And why haven't you mentioned him yet?"

"When do we get to meet him?"

"How did you—"

"Girls, girls." Edie held up her hands, and both girls fell silent, although they continued leaning forward in the booth eagerly, desperate for details. This was a big deal, and Edie knew it—as far as her daughters were aware, she hadn't shown any interest in a man since their father had died. They didn't know that for the past twenty years, amid the sea-breeze days and starry nights, she had been slowly falling in love with Henry Turner.

As she pictured him, a gentle smile spread across her face, and she clasped her hands on the table, fingers entwined. As she did so, she caught sight of her wedding ring—the simple gold band that hadn't left her finger for fifty-three years—and then her hand automatically trailed to her throat. She untucked the gold chain she always wore and stroked Johnny's ring, always nestled near her heart, where it belonged.

Where he belonged, and forever would.

"It's true," Edie said softly, tucking her husband's ring back beneath her blouse. "I have met someone— well, I met him twenty years ago, to be more precise.

But recently, things have begun to change. I think…" Her voice trailed off as she tried to give voice to the feelings that had been rising inside her for some time.

"Oh my." Karina pressed a hand to her chest and leaned back against the booth. She nudged her sister in the side. "I think our mother is in love."

Her eyes filled with tears, and she grabbed a napkin to blot them away. "Sorry," she said with a sniffle, twisting the napkin around in her fingers. "I'm just happy for you. I know Dad would give you his blessing without a second thought—he wouldn't have wanted you to be alone for this long."

She dabbed at her eyes once more, then reached across the table to squeeze her mother's hand. "This is wonderful news, Mom."

At the mention of their father, Laurie lowered her gaze to the table, fingers gripping the edge as she took a deep breath. When she spoke, her voice was trembling. "I feel the same way, Mom, and I want nothing more than for you to be happy. I just…"

She broke off for a moment and closed her eyes, composing herself. "I just wish it didn't need to be this way, you know? You and Dad were the most amazing couple, and I speak for all three of us kids when I say that we always looked up to you and hoped to one day have a relationship as solid and loving as yours. Dad dying as young as he did… it just wasn't fair."

"No. It wasn't." Edie leaned across the table to grip her daughter's hand. "We never know when the people we love the most will leave us, which is why we need to make every second with them count. You know that saying, the one about never going to bed angry?"

When the girls nodded, she laughed. "Your father and I never believed in that—sometimes we went to bed raging mad at each other, usually over something silly that we wouldn't remember a week later. But we always, *always* apologized when we were wrong, and respected each other's differences. It's true that the love we had only comes around once in a lifetime, if you're lucky enough to find that person who fits you perfectly—but sometimes we're also lucky enough to find love again. Henry will never replace your father in my heart, nor does he want to. He merely wants to write a new chapter of my book with me."

As she finished speaking, Edie became aware that her daughters had suddenly straightened in the booth, their faces wary. They exchanged a quick glance, silently communicating with each other, before Karina turned back to Edie with a frown.

"Did you say Henry? You don't mean Henry Turner, do you? That miserable old man who owns the inn near your shop?"

Edie raised her eyebrows, taken aback by her daughter's frank assessment of her longtime friend and new love. Henry had walls up, yes—everyone in town knew that, although very few were privy to the sad story of his past, the young love he'd lost due to circumstances outside of his control. But Edie knew him better than probably anyone, and underneath the gruff exterior was a warm, caring, generous man who deserved better than the reputation he had.

"Oh, Mom, no," Laurie chimed in, correctly interpreting Edie's silence. "I've seen him dozens of times since you moved to the island, and not once has he ever waved hello or stopped to chat. I can't even recall a single time he's ever smiled at me on the sidewalk—the rest of the island's residents are so friendly, so welcoming. How did you ever…"

She left the rest of the sentence dangling in the air between them, and once more, Edie's daughters exchanged looks of concern.

Edie leaned back in the booth, arms crossed over her chest, and gave the girls a fierce look. "Haven't you learned yet that you can't judge a book by its cover? I'm not going to get into Henry's life story with you, because it's not mine to tell, but he erected those walls to protect himself from getting hurt again. It's a shame, too, because he has a lot to offer —and it may have taken him sixty years to start knocking those walls down, but that's something he should be commended for. It's not easy opening your heart to love again… after all, I should know."

Her daughters looked momentarily chagrinned, but then Karina leaned back in the booth with a long sigh and shook her head. "Sorry, Mom, I just don't see it. You're beautiful, and poised, and vivacious, and he walks around with a look on his face like he is perpetually smelling something unpleasant. Are you sure you aren't just…"

She stopped speaking and began chewing anxiously on her lower lip.

"Lonely?" Edie folded her hands on the table. "Is that what you wanted to say?"

Karina hesitated and glanced at her sister, who nodded. Edie sat back and crossed one leg over the other as she studied her daughters' faces. Even though she was frustrated and disappointed by their reaction to her news, she could tell that they were genuinely worried about her—and could she really fault them for that? On the contrary, it was nice to have someone looking out for her, even if she didn't need it.

"Of course I'm lonely," she said with a soft sigh, grabbing a straw from the corner of the table and threading it in and out of her fingers. "I've been lonely since your father passed away, but that's not why Henry and I are together. We're together because we have genuine feelings for each other, and that's not something that comes along every day when you've reached a certain age."

She dropped the straw and ran her fingers through her silver hair. "You girls are still young— you have your whole lives ahead of you, and hope-fully many more years of happiness with your spouses. Is it so bad that I'd like to experience that too? Only God knows how much time each of us has left, and it's up to us to make the most of it."

At this, the girls fell silent, each gazing at the table, lost in her own thoughts. Then, after a few more moments of quiet, Laurie raised her head and met her mother's eyes.

"You're right, Mom, and I'm sorry. We want every good thing in the world for you, and if Henry Turner makes you happy, well"—she took a deep breath and nodded at her sister—"then we're happy for you."

Karina nodded her agreement, and another hush fell over the table as each woman remembered the man who had loomed so large in their life, and who had been taken from them far too soon.

After a while, Edie nodded and said, "Good. Now what looks good for dinner? And since you're buying, I think I'll have dessert too."

There was a startled pause as her daughters stared at her, and then the three women broke out in spontaneous peals of laughter that immediately lightened the mood, and their hearts.

CHAPTER 7

*D*aphne flicked open the can of tuna fish and whistled for Luna, and before long, she saw the plump tabby cat slinking around the corner, eyes on her meal. She ducked out of Daphne's reach when she tried to stroke her fur and began digging into the dinner while Daphne watched her, torn between amusement and frustration at the cat's obvious ambivalence toward her. Truth be told, she would have preferred a dog, but the long hours she worked at the diner didn't leave much room for caring for herself, let alone another pet.

Once Luna had finished scarfing down her meal —and immediately disappeared again, not to be seen until breakfast—Daphne settled onto her couch, kicked off her slippers, and began rubbing her feet. The day had been long, but that wasn't why she was feeling so unsettled—or why she had spent much of last night staring at the ceiling, watching the shadows dance moonlit patterns around her and thinking of Jax.

Daphne had always been a people pleaser, and so part of her felt bad for acting so aloof toward him... while the other part continually reminded her that he deserved nothing less. The summer before Jax started college—their last summer together on the island—he had made so many plans with her for the future, so many declarations of love that he'd had no intention of keeping. When he caught the ferry to the mainland for the last time, he had held her in his arms and kissed her like he never wanted to stop, and then promised that the next time he returned, it would be with a ring and a promise.

And she never saw him again. Until yesterday, that is.

A sudden knock at the door startled her, and she gazed at it, head cocked, wondering who on earth would be visiting her at this hour, after such a long shift. She debated not opening it, but then raised herself off the couch with a sigh, slid her feet back into her slippers, and padded toward the door. A glance through the peephole had her immediately perking up, and she quickly swung open the door with a grin and greeted Tana, who was standing on her front step with a plate of chocolate chip cookies and a bottle of red wine.

"I know they won't be as good as yours," Tana said, stepping into Daphne's apartment and setting down the cookies before turning to give her friend a hug. "But I was baking up a storm today, and there's no way I can eat all of this on my own."

Daphne frowned at her as she eyed the cookies, then crossed her arms over her chest and said, "Okay, spill it. What's wrong?"

"What do you mean?"

Tana returned the frown as she headed for Daphne's kitchen to uncork the wine and dig two glasses out of the cabinet. Daphne heard the cork popping and joined her friend in the kitchen, leaning against the counter as she watched Tana pour two generous glasses and immediately raise one to her lips.

"What?" she asked again, but this time, she didn't meet Daphne's gaze.

"You never bake unless you're stressed," Daphne said, reaching for her own glass of wine. "So, like I said—spill it."

Tana hesitated for a long moment, staring into her glass and swirling the wine around absentmindedly. Finally, she looked up, meeting Daphne's gaze, and took a deep breath. "Uncle Henry has decided that once the inn opens he wants to add in a full breakfast menu, like he used to offer guests in the past, and he wants Jax to be the chef."

At the mention of Jax's name, Daphne felt her heart sink. She was still trying to process the fact that he was on the island again—now Tana was telling her that they would have to work together too? Henry and Tana had already asked Daphne to provide pastries to their guests, and even though she wouldn't always be baking them on site, she'd still be at the inn every day to drop them off—meaning she'd see Jax every day.

She sighed, long and loud, and said, "It's okay, Tana. I'm a professional—we'll be able to work together."

Tana stared at her, clearly nonplussed, and then cocked her head. "Sorry, I'm not following. Who will be able to work together?"

Daphne took a restrained sip of her wine, wishing she could chug the whole thing—and the rest of the bottle too. "Me and Jax. It's been a long time, and we're good."

Okay, that may have been a stretch, but what other choice did she have? She had blocked Jax from her heart long ago, and she supposed now was as good a time as any to prove to herself that she was over what he did to her, once and for all.

Tana set down her glass and squinted at Daphne. "Honestly, I have no idea what you're talking about."

And then it hit Daphne—of course Tana didn't understand what she was saying. She had no idea about Daphne and Jax's shared past. Even though the three of them had spent every summer together, she and Jax had decided to keep their relationship private—they were each other's most precious secret, a fragile piece of sea glass they were afraid would shatter if too many people held it in their hands. Which meant that Tana also had no idea that her brother had devastated Daphne, broken her trust and fractured her faith in other people's promises.

She cleared her throat, her mind working frantically to backpedal while her mouth hung open stupidly. Finally, she said, "I just meant we haven't seen each other for many years, so I'm sure it'll take us some time to get back into the swing of things if we're going to work together. Jax and I, we weren't as close as you and I were, Tana, so we won't be able to pick up our friendship right where it left off."

Then she took another long sip of wine to cover the awkward moment, hoping Tana would accept her explanation and move on.

Fortunately, Tana nodded, though she kept her eyes on her wine glass, which she was now moving in slow circles on the counter, as if she was lost in thought. Then she sighed, closed her eyes, and said, "I'm trying to beat around the bush, but that isn't fair to you. Daphne"—she inhaled sharply, then winced —"I know we had an agreement, and it makes me sick to have to say these words to you out loud, but Uncle Henry has made up his mind, and since he's the inn's owner, there isn't much I can do to change it. Believe me, I've tried."

She met Daphne's gaze, her eyes filled with regret. "Uncle Henry has decided that, at least for now, he won't be hiring you. It's not in the budget to have both a chef and a pastry chef, and he's decided to go with the former. I'm sorry. I'm so, so sorry." The last words came out as a whisper.

Then Tana hastened to add, "But it's only tempo-rary—Jax doesn't want the position for long; he's just planning on spending a couple months on the island to regroup and deal with some personal issues. Before he leaves, he's going to train you as his replacement, and you'll take over the official role as the chef for the Inn at Dolphin Bay. I know this isn't what we agreed on, and it pushes your timeline back a few months, but I've been thinking about it, and I think this could work better for you in the long run. The pay will be better, so you'll be able to leave the diner sooner and..."

She shook her head. "Sorry. I'm rambling, because I'm trying to make sure you understand that I would never abandon you like that. I also want to make sure you don't hate me." She hesitated, then added, in a small voice, "Do you?"

While her friend was speaking, Daphne's mind was whirling, trying to keep up with everything she was hearing. Her first instinct had been to be furious, but when she took a step back and thought about it with a clear head, Tana was right—if Daphne's ultimate goal was to find a career for herself outside of the diner, then this was a more promising offer. Baking was Daphne's passion, though—could she really see herself as a chef? And more importantly, was that what she wanted?

Forget about the fact that Jax would be training her. Daphne couldn't fully wrap her head around *that* one right now, and until she stepped into that kitchen with him, she had no plans of even trying.

All of these thoughts were running through her

head as she stared at Tana without really seeing her, and it was only when Tana stepped forward and placed a hand on her arm that Daphne was drawn back into the present—and into the look of panic on her friend's face.

"You hate me, don't you?" Tana said, her voice catching. "Oh, Daphne, I don't know what to—"

"No." Daphne reached out to squeeze her hand in reassurance. "If I'm being honest, I'm a little unsure about the whole chef thing—it's not really what I had envisioned, but you're right. This is a great opportunity, and if all goes well, I'll be putting in my notice at the diner before the weather turns cold." She grinned at Tana. "And what better early Christmas present for myself than that?"

Tana grinned back at her, looking thoroughly relieved. When she turned away to refill their glasses for a celebratory toast, Daphne gripped the edges of the counter and drew in a deep breath. Only time would tell if this would truly be a good opportunity for her—or if, once again, and like her sister Corinne didn't hesitate to point out, she was giving up on her dreams.

JAX ROCKED SLOWLY on the battered wicker chair, gazing out at the tops of the colorful umbrellas that lined the beach as far as the eye could see. He'd always loved the views from the inn's expansive front porch—the beach in front of him, its soft golden sand practically glowing in the sun; the lighthouse to his left, surrounded by tall dune grass that swayed in the gentle wind; the mainland far in the distance, the outline of its trees visible on a clear day.

But as beautiful as this island was, it had also become his prison.

It hadn't started out that way. In fact, when his mother—excuse him, *Julie*—first informed Jax and Tana that they would be spending their summers with her uncle at his inn in picturesque Dolphin Bay, he'd been ecstatic. The idea of sunny days filled with boogie boarding, beach volleyball, biking on the island's winding paths, and yes, even helping Uncle Henry out at the inn, had been nothing short of magical. His friends were by and large spending their summers in their own backyards, under the constant watchful eyes of their parents.

But he and Tana would be *free*.

And their first summer had been just that. Well, the first two weeks of it, anyway.

Then the tourists had come, with their sand toys and chairs, with their surfboards and coolers, with their excited faces. That last part had gotten to him first—the families. Mothers and fathers holding their children's hands, or playing with them in the waves, or taking them out for an ice cream cone after a long day of enjoying the summer sunshine and fresh air. Their grinning faces hadn't seemed to effect Tana, but to Jax, they were a dagger straight to the heart.

He'd never had that. He'd never experienced a true family. He and his sister were close, yes—they'd had no other choice than to lean on each other in the absence of a stable parent in their lives. They'd never known their father—he had left town when Jax was a toddler and Tana a newborn, never to be seen again. Their mother never spoke of him. He didn't even know the man's name.

And Julie had been too busy building her career to bother being a mother. Why she had kids in the first place, Jax could never figure out. Not as a kid, when he spent hours trying to wrap his head around it every time he watched her come home from a month-long gig and then immediately pack a bag for another one. Not as an adult, when he decided he never wanted to become a father. The thought struck terror in his very bones—how could he properly raise a kid if he had no idea what it meant to be a parent? The last thing he wanted was to do to his own child what his mother had done to him.

At first, those vacationing families were merely a bother. Their presence annoyed Jax as they crowded the islands, suffocating him with their happy smiles and their laughter and their *togetherness*. As he grew older, and realized what had been missing from his life, that annoyance had morphed into a feeling of being abandoned, unwanted, unloved.

The chasm it opened up inside him was a wound that could never truly be filled. Not even by Daphne, though he had loved her from the moment he laid eyes on her, when she was all gangly limbs and freckles and goofy, awkward grins. She had come close—*he* had come close. For a time, he thought he'd be able to make a family with her.

But it wasn't meant to be. Because although she was calling to him, a beautiful voice that penetrated his defenses and was a tonic to his wounded soul, there were other voices, too. And those ones were always the loudest.

The sound of footsteps crunching on gravel reached his ears, and Jax tore his gaze away from the beachgoers—and the memories they evoked—and turned his attention to the man walking up the inn's driveway toward him. He was probably around Jax's age, with dark hair that was graying at the edges and a lean, muscular frame and tanned skin that spoke of hard work and endless days in the sun. The man was carrying a small cooler at his side, and when his eyes met Jax's, he raised his hand in greeting.

"Hey, I'm Reed," he said as he reached the bottom of the porch steps. "You must be Tana's brother." He grinned up at him, a boyish smile that instantly made him look ten years younger.

Ah. The boyfriend. When Jax had found out that Tana was dating someone, his hackles were immediately raised—she'd been through a lot in the past couple of months, and he feared whoever this man was would take advantage of her vulnerability. But she seemed happy, and since arriving on the island, he'd heard nothing but good things about Reed Dawes, so Jax was more than willing to give him a chance.

He stood too, nodding at Reed. "Nice to meet you."

Reed held up the cooler, then jabbed his thumb over his shoulder in the direction of the beach. "I have a few hours off work, and it's a beautiful day, so I thought I'd head down to the water for a little while. Would you like to join me? Tana's been talking about you pretty much nonstop, and she's dying for the two of us to meet."

Jax considered the offer. Truth be told, he was exhausted. The ordeal of the past couple of years—heck, the ordeal of the past couple of *decades*—had left him drained of energy. He hadn't realized how bone-tired he was until he'd arrived in Dolphin Bay and finally had a chance to decompress. Running a restaurant was more than a full-time job; it was a way of life. Early mornings, late nights, never a chance to fully relax when he was constantly being pulled in twenty directions. What he wanted right now, what he craved, was solitude. And having an awkward conversation with the man his sister was falling in love with definitely did not qualify.

But this man meant something to Tana, so was there really any decision to be made?

"That sounds great," Jax said, hiding the reluctance he felt.

He turned off the music he'd been listening to and slid his phone into his pocket, then headed down the steps to shake hands with Reed. The two men walked shoulder to shoulder as they left the inn's property and approached the winding dirt path that led down to the beach. Jax averted his eyes from the vacationers making their way up the path opposite him—in particular a young couple with a pair of kids who were talking a mile a minute and clinging to their parents' hands, their cheeks glowing with happiness and sticky from the cherry popsicles they were sucking on.

Not until they were out of sight did Jax realize that Reed was giving him an odd, almost expectant look—had he been talking? He cast his mind back frantically, trying to piece together the background noise that he only now realized had been Reed trying to have a conversation with him.

Reed laughed at the sight of Jax's bewildered expression. "I was just asking if you were enjoying being back on the island. Don't worry about it—I know you've had a lot on your plate the last few days, and it always takes me a while to adjust whenever I start a vacation. I'm always running through a thousand things in my head the first day I have a chance to relax—if you can call it that."

"Yeah, sorry, I guess I'm a little out of sorts. It's strange being back here after so many years. Seeing what happened to my uncle's inn was difficult, and then running into people I haven't seen for such a long time…"

Jax's voice trailed off as he thought of Daphne,

the anger in her eyes and the flush to her cheeks as she confronted him on the inn's porch. He had accepted the end of their relationship long ago, of course—at the time, it had been inevitable, and necessary—but she would never stop being the one that got away.

When he pulled himself out of his thoughts once more, he saw that Reed was watching him from the corner of his eye as they reached the end of the trail and stepped into the pillow-soft sand. There was a beat of silence as he seemed to be waiting for Jax to speak, but when he declined to finish his sentence, Reed merely nodded and headed toward the water's edge. He slid his feet out of his shoes and kicked off his socks, then lowered himself easily to the sand while Jax followed suit, grateful that Reed hadn't pressed him for more information. He rarely thought about those days, out of necessity. And self-preservation.

"So Tana tells me you're an amazing chef," Reed said as he tucked his knees up to his chin and stared out at the water. A few feet away from them, a group of teenage boys in swim trunks and T-shirts were tossing around a Frisbee, clapping and cheering every time someone had to dive into the waves to retrieve it. "She was absolutely raving about your food. Which makes me feel terrible, of course, since I can barely throw together a ham and cheese sandwich without managing to screw it up."

Reed grinned at Jax, who returned the smile. He could already feel himself warming up to his sister's new boyfriend, which surprised him. Even though he and Derek had enjoyed an easygoing, friendly relationship, it had taken Jax some time before he fully accepted him. Thanks to the transient nature of their childhood, he was, admittedly and to Tana's great dislike, more overprotective of her than most older brothers.

"Tana and I had to make our own dinners a lot when we were growing up, and after a while I got tired of peanut butter and jelly or scrambled eggs," Jax said with a shake of his head. "When I was around twelve, I started experimenting with recipes of my own, and somewhere along the way, it moved from a hobby to a passion. I'm much more at home in the kitchen than anywhere else."

"That's how I feel about the water," Reed said, gesturing toward the rippling blue-gray ocean. "I moved to Dolphin Bay to help take care of my mother after my father passed away, and I'll be honest, I was more than a little unsure about this place at first. For a guy in his early twenties, it can seem like a prison—not a decent bar or nightclub in sight."

He laughed. "Then I discovered how I felt when I was out on the water—the serenity I felt, the strength, the connection to nature. It was like a drug. But I couldn't bum around on my kayak all day and still earn a paycheck, so I decided to do something about it." He proceeded to describe his business to Jax before inviting him on a kayak tour of the island —which Jax readily agreed to.

As they talked, the sun rose higher in the sky and the air grew warmer, and before long, both men were wiping sweat from their brows and peeling their shirts away from their skin. One glance around the beach showed Jax that the vacationers were feeling the heat too—those who weren't bobbing up and down in the water were hidden beneath umbrellas or canopies, cool drinks in their hands. Just as he was regretting not grabbing some iced tea or lemonade before leaving the inn, he heard a popping sound and turned to find Reed opening the cooler at his side.

"Want one?" he asked Jax, pulling out a bottle of beer that was dripping with melted ice. Next he produced a bottle opener, popping off the top of the can with ease before passing it to Jax.

Jax stared down at the bottle glistening in the sun and swallowed hard against his suddenly dry throat. Then he shook his head and set the bottle on the sand between them. "No thanks, I don't drink."

The words surprised him; he rarely discussed his sobriety with anyone to avoid having to answer uncomfortable questions, and when he realized what he had done, he cringed and waited for the inevitable interest.

But Reed merely nodded, grabbed the bottle, and rummaged around in the cooler for another moment before pulling out a can of soda. "How about this?"

"Yes." Jax could hear the relief saturating his voice. "That would be great, thanks."

Then he accepted the can from Reed, and the two men took long sips of the cool drinks in unison before continuing to enjoy the balmy day, the sand between their toes, and the start of a new and unexpected friendship.

CHAPTER 8

*D*aphne set down the book she was reading at the sound of footsteps outside her apartment door, cringing as she looked around her small living room, her eyes landing on the empty takeout boxes, clothes scattered on the furniture, and dusty surfaces. Mara had called in sick at the diner all this week, leaving them short one waitress during one of the busiest times of the summer, and Sal had asked Daphne to cover some of her shifts. The past few days had been draining, leaving Daphne's feet aching and her eyes blurred with exhaustion, and when she finally came home each night, she could barely summon the energy to wash her face, let alone tidy up the apartment.

It wasn't like Luna cared—as long as the cat's

food bowl was filled on schedule, she was a happy camper. Besides, Tana wouldn't mind the mess—she was currently living in a construction zone—and no one else had dropped by Daphne's place unexpected since the last time she had a boyfriend, which was...

Daphne squinted, trying to recall when she and Brad had dated, then gave up after a moment and began gathering the empty food containers and carrying them over to the trash. The knock on the door came as soon as she stepped back into the living room, leaving her a few seconds to run her fingers through her hair to unknot it before she slapped a welcoming smile on her face and opened the door, forgetting to look through the peephole first.

And immediately realizing her mistake.

"Daphne!"

Corinne's face was crinkled in a smile as she held her arms open wide, as if expecting a hug. If Daphne couldn't remember the last time she had seen Brad, she *definitely* couldn't remember the last time she had hugged her sister. Corinne's desire for air kisses only increased as the numbers in her bank account did the same. She took a step back on instinct, but not before shooting a horrified glance into her messy apartment.

"Corinne, what are you doing here?"

Daphne had to work hard to keep the ice out of her voice. Even though she was still reeling from their last conversation, the only way she and her sister could maintain some semblance of a relationship was if they swept everything that wasn't superficial under the rug.

And then threw away the broom.

"You don't sound happy to see me." Corinne gave an airy laugh, but Daphne saw the flash of hurt in her sister's eyes, the way her hands clenched tighter around the straps of her designer purse.

She sighed and opened the door wider, resigning herself to the inevitable criticism. "Of course I am, I was just surprised to see you. Come in."

As she ushered her sister inside, she managed to toe a few cat toys under her coffee table and toss her apron from the diner onto the back of her recliner instead of leaving it in the middle of the floor, where she'd dropped it last night before immediately collapsing on the couch and falling asleep.

Corinne looked around the small space, her face crinkling even more as her smile stretched wider. "I love what you've done with the place. Very homey."

She gingerly moved aside a pile of magazines before perching on the edge of the couch, keeping her arms wrapped around herself as if Daphne's distinct lack of social status would rub off on her if she made herself too comfortable.

As if she hadn't gone to high school in threadbare secondhand clothes that Daphne took it upon herself to mend each week, just so her sister wouldn't have to be embarrassed.

"So," she said, her voice tight as she tried to rein in her annoyance, "to what do I owe the pleasure? I literally cannot remember the last time you visited the island. Oh, wait." She made a show of snapping her fingers and pursing her lips in thought. "That would have been our mother's funeral, right? But if I recall correctly, you took the next ferry back to the mainland the moment the service was over. Heaven forbid you would spend an extra second or two with the peasants."

"Daphne, stop." Corinne suddenly looked drained. "It's never enough with you, is it? I came here to see you, to tell you something exciting, but you continue to dredge up the past. You made your choice, and I made mine. Are you really going to spend the rest of your life shaming me for trying to make something of myself? Because like it or not, I'm the only sister you have—and if you continue to keep me at arm's length, eventually I'm just going to honor your wishes."

She broke off, her voice catching. "Is that really what you want?"

No. It wasn't. It desperately, desperately wasn't. They used to be so close, but some hurts became rivers too deep to cross.

Instead of answering, Daphne took a sudden interest in the chipped polish on her fingernails. She was half hoping that her sister would take the hint and leave, but Corinne remained stubbornly in place, arms folded, one leg crossed over the other, blue eyes pinned on Daphne.

Finally, she relented, looking up from her nails to say, "How's Harper?" Because as furious as Daphne was with her sister, she cared deeply for the baby's well-being... and hoped that someday she would be able to enjoy a close relationship with her.

Corinne's tense shoulders lowered a fraction, and a smile eased onto her face. "She's wonderful. Even though Raymond thinks I'm out of my mind, I'm considering letting our nanny go. Harper is only going to be a baby for a few short months, and I want to soak in every last moment with her while I can."

Daphne frowned. That was the first sensible

thing she'd heard her sister say in years. "I think that's a wonderful idea," she said, folding her hands in her lap. Then she glanced toward the kitchen, and back to her sister. "Can I get you something to drink?"

"Tea would be nice," Corinne said, then smiled at Daphne. "If it's not too much trouble."

"It's not." Daphne bustled into the kitchen to put the kettle on, grateful for the distraction. As she waited for the water to heat, she leaned against the counter, staring out into the living room and studying her sister's profile. She had always considered Corinne to be the more beautiful of the two of them, but from a distance, Daphne could see the clear similarities—the same heart-shaped face, dark blue eyes, and thick blonde hair. She ran her hands through her own hair and sighed. Maybe Corinne was right. Maybe she was too hard on herself.

When she returned a short while later with two mugs of spiced tea, Corinne was studying the photos that lined Daphne's mantel with a wistful smile. "Mom was beautiful, wasn't she?" she said, pointing to one of their mother in her youth. She had fully embraced the flower child look at the time, with her off-the-shoulder white blouse and billowing tie-dyed skirt. Her hair was almost to her waist, and her face was alight with happiness and a youthful glow that had turned sallow as time marched on and life took its toll. The woman Daphne said goodbye to on a windy March day looked nothing like that laughing girl.

"She was," Daphne murmured, joining her sister at the mantel. The two women stood shoulder to shoulder as they gazed at their mother's face, neither speaking, both lost in memories of a life that had been riddled with heartbreak.

When she could stand the silence—and the memories—no longer, Daphne cleared her throat and said, "So, you said you had some exciting news? Don't tell me, Raymond got another promotion."

Corinne blinked several times as she processed the interruption to her thoughts, then tore her gaze away from the photographs. "No, nothing like that. I have exciting news for *you*."

"For me?" Daphne was taken aback. She had no inkling what her sister could be referring to, and she was almost afraid to find out.

When she saw Daphne's expression, Corinne laughed. "I said it was exciting news, Daph. No one died." She swept her eyes over Daphne's face, only this time, Daphne didn't feel like her sister was silently scrutinizing her. Then Corinne inhaled sharply, pausing for a dramatic, prolonged moment before announcing, like she was about to tell a kid he could meet Santa Claus, "I found you a date!"

"A what?" Daphne gaped at her sister, certain she had misheard.

"A date." Corinne's smile was self-satisfied, and any trace of goodwill Daphne was feeling toward her instantly evaporated. "With a man I met while our house was being renovated. He's amazing, Daphne— smart, successful, *gorgeous*." She nudged her sister in the hip. "He's a true catch, and when I met him, I immediately thought of you. After our conversation at my house the other day, I got to thinking about him again, and I decided to give him a call to see if he'd be interested. And he was."

She crossed her arms over her chest smugly. "So when you fall deeply in love and get married, you can thank me."

Why, in that moment, Jax's face flashed through Daphne's mind, she would never know. She immediately squashed him back down, then glared at her sister. "Why in the world would you think I wanted you to set me up on a date with a complete stranger? I am capable of finding my own dates, thank you very much."

"I know you are." Corinne shook her head. "You

are fun and beautiful and kind-hearted, and any man would be lucky to have you. But for reasons I'll never understand, you barely put yourself out there. When's the last time you had a boyfriend? No, scratch that—when's the last time you had a date?"

"Brad." Daphne said the name emphatically, still frantically casting her mind back over the years, trying to remember when she'd last seen him. Sal's Diner had been undergoing some renovations at the time, something to do with water damage in the kitchen, and that had been right around the time when Mara had started, and she was now twenty-six, so... ten years ago?

"Oh my." The words escaped from Daphne's mouth before she could stop them. Had it really been that long?

"See what I mean?" her sister asked softly. "Mom's gone, Daphne. She has been for years. Why don't you let yourself be happy for a change?"

Daphne barely heard her—she was too busy trying to work out when she had become so lonely. Long before her mother died, that much she knew. And probably before she met Jax and experienced her first heartbreak, too. The sad truth was that Daphne had been alone for most of her life, and after living through disappointment after disappointment hand-delivered by the people who were supposed to care for her the most, eventually she had begun to believe that she deserved nothing less.

"Come on," Corinne pressed. She hesitated a moment before leaning forward and taking Daphne's hand. "It's one date, Daph. The worst that will come of it is that a nice guy will take you out for a meal. And the best that will come of it?" She shrugged. "No one can answer that, but don't you want to find out?"

～

"ANOTHER DAY IN THE BOOKS," Reed said to Kelly with a sigh as they finished cleaning out the row of kayaks glistening in the waning sunlight. "If things get much busier, I'm going to have to hire someone else to help with the tours. As it is, I'm out on the water eight times a day—if this keeps up much longer, I'm not going to be able to use my arms."

He winced as he stretched his aching muscles, his mind on the long, hot shower he planned to take the minute he stepped into his house. He and Tana had seen each other every night since their first official date on the beach, but tonight, she was planning to work on building a new website for the inn, having convinced Henry that he needed to move out of the dark ages and start accepting online bookings.

The old man had looked at her like she'd grown two heads, but any argument he was gearing up for was stopped in its tracks when Edie arrived at the inn and wound her arm around his waist. Henry had gazed at her adoringly before telling a stunned Tana that she could do whatever she wanted; then, the two of them had strolled out the inn's front door, arm in arm, heading for the boardwalk to enjoy hot fudge sundaes and the sunset on their favorite bench overlooking the water.

His mother had looked so happy that it made Reed's heart ache.

Then his thoughts turned to Tana, and he smiled. She was a special woman, no doubt about that. And if he was being honest with himself, he knew that she was much, much more than that. For the first time in his life, he was beginning to understand what it felt like to fall in love. He spent most days thinking of her—the way the corners of her mouth crinkled when she smiled, the laugh lines around her beautiful brown eyes, the secure feeling of her hand in his.

Even though he hoped she felt the same way, he couldn't stop the arrow of terror that shot straight through his heart every time he thought of Derek, the man she'd spent more than half of her life with. He didn't deserve Tana; that much was certain. But if he walked back into Tana's life today and begged for her forgiveness, what would she do? Who would she choose?

The idea that it wouldn't be him was nauseating, and a bigger part of him than he cared to admit feared that he was putting his heart on the line only to have it squashed under her pretty little foot.

"Everything okay?"

Reed was pulled out of his thoughts by Kelly, who was standing a few feet away from him at the cash register, totaling the receipts for the day and eyeing him with concern. When their gazes met, she smiled coyly and began toying with a strand of her long hair, twirling it around her fingers before adjusting her bikini top.

Inwardly, Reed sighed. *Here we go again.*

He'd tried being patient, tried letting her down easy, but the woman was persistent—and annoying. If she didn't quit the flirtatious behavior, he was going to have no choice but to tell her to find a job elsewhere, something he hadn't yet followed through with because full-time, year-round help was scarce on an island as small as Dolphin Bay.

"Everything's fine," he said gruffly, grabbing a surfboard. He tossed it onto his shoulder and entered the hut, careful to avoid bumping into her, before mounting it on the back wall along with the others. He began heading outside to grab another, but Kelly stopped him with a hand on his wrist.

"It doesn't seem that way." She gave his wrist a squeeze and widened her eyes. "You know you can tell me anything, right?" Winking at him, she added, "Having female troubles?"

Yes, he wanted to say. *With you.*

But instead, he merely shook his head and said, "Nope. All is well on that front. My girlfriend and I are solid, thanks."

"Girlfriend?" Kelly's face fell. "You don't mean that woman who visited you here the other day, do you? The one with the picnic basket?" She glanced down at her bikini top, once more adjusting the straps and bottom band, and then flicked her long red hair over her shoulders. "She was a little frumpy, don't you think?"

"Frumpy?" Reed spluttered, his cheeks heating with anger. "Tana's the most beautiful woman I've ever encountered—no competition."

"Oh, come on." Kelly folded her arms over her chest. "A man like you could have any woman he wants. *Any* woman." She took a step toward him, her eyes filled with resolve. "I know I've probably been a little vague about it, because I'm not usually one to be bold about my feelings, but"—she took a deep breath—"I think there's something here." She gestured between the two of them. "And I'd really love to go out on a date with you sometime."

"Kelly." Reed blew out a frustrated breath. "You're really putting me in a bad position here, okay? I'm your boss, and moreover, I'm just not interested. So please, if you can't set aside your feelings and behave more professionally around here, then I'm going to have to let you go."

"Excuse me, are you still open for the day? My wife and I would like to rent two kayaks."

Kelly and Reed both gave a start at the sound of the man's voice, and Reed swung around to find a middle-aged couple standing at the hut's window, which Kelly had forgotten to close for the evening. The woman looked uneasy as she glanced from Reed to Kelly and back again, then she tugged on her husband's sleeve and whispered, "Honey, I think we're interrupting something here," loud enough for everyone to hear.

"No." Reed shook his head emphatically as Kelly opened her mouth to speak. "You aren't interrupting anything at all. And I'm sorry, but we're closed for the day—but please, come back tomorrow, and we'd be happy to rent out the kayaks, or you could even consider joining one of our group tours of the island."

The couple appeared interested in Reed's offer, so he stepped outside to speak with them, leaving Kelly alone in the hut, her arms crossed tightly over her chest and a thoughtful expression on her face.

CHAPTER 9

"I hate you. I hate you I hate you I hate you," Tana said, smacking the bottom of the computer mouse against the desk repeatedly before lowering her head into her hands and groaning in frustration. Why, why, *why* did she offer to build a website for the inn? She had exactly zero experience in web design, or computers in general—Emery loved to call her technologically illiterate, and even though Tana always protested, she silently agreed with her daughter's assessment each and every time.

So naturally, designing a website from scratch was the perfect job for her.

"But I love you." Daphne's voice was teasing as she stepped through the inn's front door and grinned at Tana. "Remind me not to stop by uninvited anymore." She dropped her purse on the floor and approached the desk, peering over Tana's shoulder at the computer screen. "What's all this?"

"*This* is my worst nightmare. And yours, too, if you don't run away from here fast." She gestured at the partially built website, which was, admittedly, a disaster.

Build a custom website in under an hour! That's what the host site had said. It lied.

"Here, let me." Daphne laughed softly, then nudged Tana out of the chair before perching on it and staring intently at the screen. With a few clicks of the mouse, she began rearranging icons on the screen, swapping out the garish blue background that Tana had accidentally chosen for something softer and more reminiscent of the ocean, and added the inn's logo to the top of the page.

"Wow." Tana shook her head in amazement. "I've been sitting here for five hours and haven't accomplished that much. Daphne, you are a woman of many talents. Forget about baking; *this* could be your next career."

"I'd hate sitting in a chair all day," Daphne said, her eyes still on the website in progress. "I need freedom.

But"—another three clicks of the mouse and a customizable calendar for bookings popped up on the screen—"a couple years ago, Sal decided he wanted a website for the diner but was too cheap to hire an actual designer. So I volunteered for the job—I could always use the extra cash, and it gave me a chance to exercise my brain for a change. I'm happy to help you."

"Thank you." Tana exhaled loudly; she could feel the relief written all over her face. "I owe you, big time."

"Good." Daphne swiveled around in her chair to face her. "Then I have my first job for you: to go on a date in my place."

Tana's eyes widened with excitement. "A date? Who, when, where?" She leaned against the desk and folded her arms, staring at her friend intently. "I want every single detail, and you better not leave anything out."

Daphne groaned and pressed her hands to her cheeks. "I don't *have* any details. I've never even seen him. Corinne said she'd met this amazing guy and wanted to introduce me to him. Of course I was going to say no, but then something came over me, and before I knew it, I was agreeing to go out with him. I don't even know his name! Corinne wouldn't tell me because she wanted the date to be totally blind."

Daphne slumped back in the chair and shook her head. "I don't know what I was thinking. I'm so out of my element here." She gave Tana an imploring look. "You'll go in my place, won't you?"

"Only if I can bring Reed with me." Tana laughed, then patted her friend on the shoulder. "Besides, I think it sounds like fun. What's the worst that could happen? You'll go to dinner with the guy and then never see him again."

"Now you sound like my sister." Daphne winced. "She was very persuasive."

"That sounds like a good thing. Besides, you just might meet the man of your dreams. Wouldn't it be funny if it's someone you already know? Like Jax? Can you imagine walking into the restaurant and seeing him waiting for you?"

"Jax?" Daphne gaped at Tana. "Why in the world would you say a thing like that?"

She looked so horrorstricken that Tana cocked her head in confusion. "Daphne, I'm kidding—I was just using my brother as an example since you two have known each other from the time we were kids. How would Corinne have run into Jax in the first place? He's been living in Philadelphia for years."

"You're right, sorry." Daphne let out a shaky laugh. "I think I'm a little worked up about this date, that's all. It's messing with my head." She glanced around the inn's foyer. "Where is Jax, anyway? I haven't seen him around town much."

"He stays around here, mostly." Tana sighed as she thought about her brother. He was still the same friendly, easygoing guy as ever, but ever since he'd returned to the island, she could sense a sadness lurking underneath the surface of his smile. Which she supposed was to be expected, given the loss of his restaurant. But still, she couldn't help but feel that something else was going on, something she wasn't privy to.

"I think he needs a break," she added as Daphne watched her closely. "He's had a rough go of it lately, but I'm sure he'll come out of his shell soon enough. He's making friends, though—Reed asked him to stop over tonight for pizza and to watch the Red Sox game on TV. And don't forget, you'll be seeing plenty of him soon enough—remember, he's going to be training you to take over for him as chef here at the inn."

"Oh, I haven't forgotten." Daphne glanced away, returning her focus to the computer screen. "Now why don't we spend a little more time working on the website, and then you can come back to my place and help me pick out an outfit for my date. I spend most of my days wearing a food-stained apron, and I can't remember the last time I dug a dress out of my closet."

"Sounds like a plan." Tana dragged a chair over to the desk to join her friend. "And again, thank you for —oh!" She waved to Jax as he descended the stairs from his bedroom on the inn's upper floor. "Speak of the devil. Daphne and I were just talking about you."

Jax's eyes shifted to Daphne and then back again. "Nothing too terrible, I hope," he joked.

"Only about what a jerk you are," Tana teased, then grinned at Daphne only to find her friend staring hard at the computer, her brow furrowed in concentration. She barely acknowledged Jax with a distracted smile before returning to her task, the mouse flying across the screen a mile a minute as she clicked furiously.

Her brother watched Daphne's face for a moment, then turned to Tana with his trademark mischievous grin. "I'm off to hang out with your boyfriend now—are you nervous?"

"Only that he's going to take one look at you and run for the hills." Tana shook her head. "At least you're not Mom. Then I'd really be in trouble."

"Yeah, Julie has that effect on people, doesn't she?" Jax's smile slipped, and he shoved his hands into the pockets of his jeans. "I'm headed to Reed's place now, so I'll see you later, okay?" He hesitated, then turned to Daphne. "See ya, Daphne."

She raised her hand in a curt goodbye wave, never taking her eyes from the screen. Tana watched the awkward exchange in confusion. As children, and later teenagers, she, Daphne, and Jax were a tight trio—spending their days and nights exploring the island, goofing off on the beach, and eating greasy burgers and fries on the boardwalk while inventing stories about the tourists who walked by. She couldn't remember any kind of tension between them twenty-five years ago, so why now, after all these years, did they seem so uncomfortable in each other's presence?

Before she could ponder this strange turn of events further, Daphne turned the computer screen toward her, face lit up in a triumphant grin. "There. It's not perfect yet, but what do you think about this as a rough template for the home page?"

"Oh, Daph, I don't know what to say." Tana stared at the website in amazement. "I love it, and I know Uncle Henry will too."

Daphne had chosen a beautiful script font for the

banner, along with a photograph that perfectly showcased the breathtaking view of the ocean and lighthouse from the inn's front porch. The entire website was designed with soft blues and tans, and Daphne had arranged the photos Tana had taken of the inn's interior—pre-construction, for now, and as flattering as she could make them—into a slideshow that also displayed the story Tana had written about the inn's history.

Her heart swelled as she glanced up from the computer and looked around the beautiful family inn, which was still a construction zone but would soon shine like it had for so many decades, a place of welcome and respite for the families who had chosen to vacation here year after year, making memories that would last them a lifetime. Tana and Jax had plenty of their own memories here too—and she could scarcely wait for the ones that she had yet to make.

For Tana, the grand reopening of the Inn at Dolphin Bay couldn't come soon enough.

～

REED GAZED LONGINGLY at the pair of large pizzas sitting on the coffee table, piping hot and perfectly cheesy. Jax wasn't set to arrive for another ten minutes, but the delivery guy had showed up early, and it was all he could do to stop himself from snagging a slice... or three.

But it would be rude to start eating dinner without the arrival of his dinner guest. Right?

Yes. Yes, it definitely would.

Reed glanced at the clock with a sigh. Nine minutes and thirty-seven seconds. He supposed he could make it, but in all fairness, being out on the water all day made him ravenous, and today had been especially grueling. The kayak tours had been nonstop, and as much as Reed hated to admit it, he didn't have as much stamina in his forties as he did when he was in his twenties. But still, he wouldn't trade his time on the water for anything in the world.

Anything other than time spent with Tana, of course. A few months ago, the idea that he would have found a woman he could imagine spending the rest of his life with was laughable. His lack of luck in the dating world had been fine in his twenties and thirties—he figured he still had plenty of time to find the one. But when forty hit and he still went to bed alone each night, he started to resign himself to the possibility that he may never fall in love.

Then Tana had walked into his life and turned his world upside down. Suddenly, the things he had given up on envisioning—a partner to experience the ups and downs of life with, a hand to hold in the good times and the bad—no longer seemed so unattainable. He found himself daydreaming about the home they would build together, the meals they would share, the day-to-day mundane things in life that everyone took for granted.

He was daydreaming about a future. Their future.

Whistling to himself, Reed flicked on the television and flipped through the channels until he came to the Red Sox game. Once he and Jax had gotten to talking, they realized they shared a love—an obsession, really—with the game, and Jax readily accepted an invitation to his place to watch the next one. It was a good opportunity for him to get to know Tana's brother—Jax was important to her, which meant he was important to Reed too. Besides, Jax could use a friend or two on the island, and if Reed had learned anything from his mother, it was that the key to a fulfilling life was making connections with others. Edie was the perfect example of kindness, and she had taught Reed and his sisters to be welcoming to everyone, stranger or not.

He sank onto the couch with a groan and turned

up the volume, then gave the pizza another longing look before focusing his attention on the start of the game. The first batter was approaching the plate when Reed heard a knock on the door, and he called out, "It's open, come on in," his eyes never leaving the television.

The door opened with a soft click as the batter swung and missed—and Reed groaned along with the crowd. "Hey, grab a seat and let's crack open these bad boys," he said, gesturing in the vague direction of the pizza as the pitcher prepared to lob the ball toward the plate once more. This time, the batter struck gold, with an arcing swing that hit the ball with a *crack* and sent it flying into the stands as the crowd went wild.

"Did you see that?" Reed said, finally tearing his eyes from the screen to greet Jax. "That was a heck of a—"

And then he stopped short when he saw that his visitor wasn't Jax at all, or anyone else he could have been expecting.

"Hi." Kelly's voice was soft as she approached the couch. Reed stiffened as he caught a whiff of her perfume. "Can I speak to you for a moment?"

She hovered over him, the trace of a smile playing across her lips. When she saw Reed hesitate, she laughed. "It's about the job, Reed. I wanted to give you something, and it couldn't wait until tomorrow."

Scratching his chin, Reed frowned at her. "So you decided to come to my house? How did you even know where I live?" He swiped his finger over his phone, wondering if he had accidentally left it on silent and expecting to see a missed call from her— but the screen was blank other than a text from Jax a few minutes ago that said *On my way*.

"Doesn't everyone know where everyone else lives on the island?" Kelly said, tucking a strand of hair behind her ear. "Anyway." She glanced at the unopened pizza boxes, then around the empty apartment. "I hope I'm not intruding on anything, but like I said, it's important and couldn't wait."

"Okay, sure." Reed muted the television and gestured for her to sit down. "What can I do for you?"

Kelly took a deep breath, then reached into her purse and pulled out a small piece of paper before passing it to Reed. He lowered his eyes to the page and quickly read what she had written on it: *Effective this evening, I am no longer an employee of Dolphin Bay Adventures*. Then he read it again, just to make sure he'd gotten it right the first time, before squinting at her.

"You're quitting?"

"I am."

"Oh, okay." Reed leaned back against the couch cushion and ran a hand through his hair. This wasn't an ideal time to lose his only employee, but he supposed he could make do for a few days until he hunted down a replacement. "Well, thanks for all the work you've put in. You were an asset to the company, and I'd be happy to write a recommendation for you or act as a reference for any future employers."

"Thank you, that would be wonderful." Kelly scooted closer to him on the couch. "There's just one more thing."

Reed, who was already mentally composing the job description he would post around town and on the internet first thing in the morning, didn't realize she had spoken again, or that she had moved even closer to him... until he turned his head and their lips met.

He also didn't realize that she'd left the door open, and that someone else was watching.

CHAPTER 10

"So here it is. Make yourself at home—she's all yours now."

Uncle Henry leaned heavily on his cane and waved his good hand around the inn's kitchen, a familiar room where Jax had spent much of his time during his summers on the island. He had developed a bond with Bennet, his uncle's former chef, a kind-hearted bear of a man with a perpetual smile and a cheerful singing voice that filled the kitchen whenever he worked. Bennet had known about Jax's interest in cooking and developing recipes of his own, and he often allowed him to help create the breakfast menus for the inn's guests. Jax credited him as one of his inspirations and role models, and he had been heartbroken to learn that his uncle had been forced to lay Bennet off years ago, when the inn was plagued with money woes.

"It just doesn't seem like the same place without him," Jax said, running his fingertips along the marble countertops that were nicked from decades of use.

He could still picture Bennet's hands flashing through the air as he expertly rotated between the oven, stovetop, counters, and refrigerator while preparing a scrumptious morning meal. The man could multitask with the best of them—never was a muffin burned, an omelet stuck to the griddle, or a strip of bacon over-crisped. He had even prepared fresh orange juice for the guests each morning, cutting the ripe fruit in half and hand-squeezing it into the pitcher; sometimes, for an extra kick, he added pineapple juice too.

On those days, Jax and Tana would sneak two glasses of it out of the kitchen—but not before adding two generous scoops of vanilla ice cream into the juice to make a float—and then enjoy their treats down by the water, slurping them happily while the seagulls circled overhead.

"It isn't." A look of sadness flashed across Uncle Henry's face; he instinctively knew who Jax was reminiscing about without having to hear Bennet's name. "That was one of the saddest days of my life, having to let him go." His great-uncle suddenly looked even older as he leaned heavily on his cane. "He was a good chef, and an even better man. We were lucky to have him for as long as we did."

"What happened to him?" Jax asked, now running his hands along the gleaming stainless-steel appliances. Over the past few nights, when sleep eluded him, as it so often did, he'd taken it upon himself to sneak down to the kitchen and quietly scrub away the years of grime that had accumulated. A fresh coat of soft blue paint by the crew still hard at work on the inn had added to the overall effect, and the result was a stunning space that looked brand-new. To his surprise, Jax even found himself excited to roam the expansive kitchen while envisioning himself behind the counter once more.

"I have no idea." Uncle Henry ran the fingers of his good hand down his wrinkled cheek. "Last I heard he'd taken whatever job he could find on the mainland. We kept in touch for a while, but it was just too painful, for both of us."

He cleared his throat, suddenly looking embarrassed, as if he had divulged too much. "Look at me, getting all wistful," he said with a gruff laugh. "Edie must be rubbing off on me." Then he thumped his cane against the floor once, changing the subject. "Like I said, the kitchen is all yours now. Do with it as you wish." He gave Jax a curt nod, then limped from the room.

Jax pulled out a chair at the small kitchen table tucked away in the corner of the room, slumping into it with a sigh before running his hands through his hair. According to Luke, the place would be up and running again in a matter of weeks. Tana was already working on the new website, which featured an online booking system to help bring Uncle Henry out of the dark ages, and word was beginning to spread around the island—and further—that the beautiful old place would soon be opening her doors to guests once more. And if the inn was ready, that meant Jax needed to be too—but this morning, he was having a hard time focusing on even the simplest of tasks.

He was even more sleep-deprived than usual. And it was all Reed's fault.

Jax's neck burned with anger as he remembered the image that had greeted him when he poked his head inside Reed's open front door, a six-pack of soda swinging from his hand, eager to relax and watch the Red Sox dominate the competition. The television had already been tuned to the game—Jax could hear the announcer's voice as he walked up Reed's front steps. But Reed hadn't been watching it.

He'd been too busy kissing another woman.

Jax had backed out of the doorway in shock before Reed noticed his presence and practically jogged down the street. Once he was a safe distance away, he'd shot Reed a quick text saying he was feeling unwell and wouldn't be able to make it to his house after all.

And then he had spent hours pacing the island's streets, trying to figure out what to do.

Only after the streetlights had blinked on and the tourists had returned to their hotels and rental houses for the night did Jax return home, his entire body filled with dread as he crunched over the inn's gravel driveway before making his way up the cobblestone sidewalk. He paused at the bottom of the porch, his eyes on his sister, who had her back to him as she slowly rocked in her favorite wicker chair, her head tipped up to the starlit sky.

"Hey," she'd said, smiling gently when she saw him. "How was the game? Did you and Reed have a good time?"

He should have told her the truth right then. In fact, he was planning on it.

Right up until he saw the sparkle of happiness in her eyes. At that moment, he felt sick.

"It was great," he managed to choke out. "The Sox lost, though."

"Bummer." Tana patted the chair next to her, then waved her hand toward the glass of wine she'd been sipping. "Care to join me?"

"No thanks." Jax stretched his arms over his head and faked a wide yawn. "I'm beat. I'm just going to hit the sack, if that's okay with you."

"Suit yourself."

Tana lifted her glass to her lips, then rested it back on her lap as she gazed at him. Her hair was blowing softly around her face in the breeze lifting up from the ocean, and her eyes were half-cast in shadow from the shifting moonlight. A smile played across her lips, the sight of which nearly broke Jax's heart.

"I just wanted to thank you," she said, "for taking the time to get to know Reed. It's hard for me, putting myself out there again after everything that's happened. Knowing you like Reed as much as I do..." She took a deep breath. "Well, that means a lot."

Then she'd turned her face back up to the night

sky, leaving Jax standing on the porch, his hands balled into fists at his sides.

When he woke up this morning, he'd vowed to tell her the truth. But she was nowhere to be found, and instead of looking for her, Jax had taken the coward's approach, hiding himself away in the kitchen, the place that had always represented safety and home to him.

He'd already had to watch his sister's heart be broken once this year. He couldn't stand there and see it happen again—maybe, this time, permanently.

REED STOOD inside the hut that served as the main office for Dolphin Bay Adventures, shielding his eyes from the harsh midday sun and working his way slowly through the line of customers who were waiting patiently for their kayak, surfboard, and paddleboard rentals. Kelly's absence meant that he was way understaffed, and he'd already been forced to cancel the day's kayak tours in order to accommodate the rental side of the business, which was, in itself, a full-time gig. He'd been greeting a constant stream of customers from the moment he turned the key in the lock that morning, and he was exhausted —but also incredibly grateful for the distraction.

Every time he thought about what happened last night, he felt physically sick to his stomach.

Not to mention angry. Very, very angry.

After the few seconds it had taken for the shock to wear off and for Reed to gather his wits about him, he broke the kiss with Kelly and stared at her, wide-eyed with shock. "What are you doing?" he demanded, pushing himself away from her to the furthest corner of the couch.

She brushed her fingertips over her mouth and gazed back at him, her lips turned up in a sly smile. "It's okay, remember? I turned in my notice—you're no longer my boss, which means we can do this and not feel weird about it."

She reached for him again, but he pushed her hand away, leaving it hanging in the air between them. "What's wrong?" she asked, her smile dimming. "I thought this was what you wanted."

Reed merely gaped at her, lost for words, as his mind frantically replayed every conversation they'd ever had. He'd never—*never*—shown interest in her; in fact, he'd actively discouraged her advances and flirtations, and he'd declined to accompany her to events outside of work, even though she'd asked him several times.

"Why would you think that?" he finally spluttered. Panic was beginning to set in as he realized that he would have to tell Tana that he had, however inadvertently, kissed another woman. After what her husband had done to her, after how he had betrayed her trust, how would she ever even begin to understand?

Kelly tucked a strand of hair behind her ear and crossed one leg over the other before folding her hands primly in her lap. "You told me that nothing could happen between us because you were my boss, meaning that if you aren't my boss, something could happen." She said the words calmly, coolly, as if this were the most logical conclusion in the world.

"I said nothing of the sort." Reed stood, folding his arms over his chest as he stared down at her. "I told you I wasn't interested in pursuing a relationship—anything I mentioned about you being an employee was an afterthought. You need to go, Kelly."

He strode over to the door, which she had left open, and peered outside into the darkening sky. At least Jax hadn't seen this debacle—Reed needed to speak to Tana before anyone else could.

A flush crept up Kelly's cheeks as she rose from the couch and approached Reed, whose hand was now braced on the doorframe as he waited for her to leave. "I wish you'd reconsider," she whispered, resting her hand on his forearm, ignoring the way he immediately tensed under her touch. "There could really be something here."

"There couldn't." Reed's voice was steel. "I'm in love with someone else. Please, Kelly, just… leave."

And finally, she had.

Mercifully, Jax had chosen that moment to text Reed to tell him that he wouldn't be able to make it over to watch the game after all, leaving Reed to collapse onto the couch and drop his head into his hands. He stayed like that for a long time as the television blared and the pizza grew cold, envisioning the expression of devastation—of betrayal—on Tana's face when he told her what had happened.

Would she believe him?

He would have to wait until this evening to find out. As soon as dusk fell and he closed up for the night, he planned to head straight to the inn and tell Tana everything that had happened.

And even though his final words to Kelly—*I'm in love with someone else*—had been unplanned, as soon as Reed said them, he knew them to be true. He had been falling for Tana since the early days of their friendship, and over the past few weeks, those feelings had grown and deepened, until he couldn't imagine a life without her by his side.

He couldn't lose her. He wouldn't.

CHAPTER 11

*D*aphne stood before the full-length mirror in her bedroom, scrutinizing her reflection from every angle. "You really think this looks okay?" she asked, turning to Tana with a grimace.

"Looks *okay*?" Tana laughed and shook her head as she folded her arms over her chest. "Daphne, you look stunning. This guy, whoever he is... you're going to knock his socks right off."

"You really think so?"

Daphne stepped closer to the mirror and adjusted one of the pins in her hair. She'd opted to sweep her long blonde hair off her face to help combat the evening's heat, and Tana had helped with her makeup, including beautiful smoky eyes she'd never been able to manage on her own. An off-the-shoulder dress in soft pink and nude peep-toe heels completed the look, and even Daphne had to admit that the outfit itself was nice—she was so used to seeing herself in a food-stained apron that she'd forgotten what she looked like in real clothes.

"I know so." Tana bent down and adjusted the hem of Daphne's dress. "I'm excited for you, and I hope you have a wonderful time."

She stepped back to give her one last admiring look. "Perfect." Then she glanced at the time on her phone before shooing Daphne out of the bedroom. "Now go! You need to catch the ferry in ten minutes, and you definitely don't want to be late. I still don't know how you're going to drive a golf cart in those heels—I can barely manage it in tennis shoes on a good day."

After nervously adjusting her hair one last time, Daphne grabbed the keys to her golf cart and hurried to the front door, Tana at her heels. "You sure you don't want to come with me?" she asked in a hopeful voice as she slung her purse over her shoulder and opened the front door. "If he turns out to be a creep, you could help me escape through the bathroom window."

"Something tells me we'd get stuck during the

attempt," Tana said with a laugh. "And when the fire department has to come and rescue you, I think all the noise they're going to make with their chainsaws is going to clue your date in to what's happening." She patted Daphne's shoulder. "Re*lax*. You're going to be fine, I promise. Call me first thing in the morning with all the details, and most importantly, have a wonderful time."

Daphne felt a rush of excitement as she blew Tana a goodbye kiss and made a beeline for her golf cart, hitching her skirt over her knees as she slid inside. She inserted the key into the slot, then paused for a moment and took a deep breath as she stared out over the horizon, where the setting sun was bathing the rippling ocean water in soft orange hues.

Despite her nerves, she was actually looking forward to the date. She couldn't remember the last time she'd eaten at a fancy restaurant; the island's dining options were mostly limited to the food stands on the boardwalk, a handful of coffee shops and bars, and, of course, the diner. She couldn't imagine the latter being the setting for a romantic dinner date, and so she was grateful to learn that her sister had made reservations at one of the swanky new restaurants that had cropped up on the mainland.

Her thoughts were on the looming date as she navigated the cart down to the harbor, where she parked in the small lot before boarding the ferry with a handful of other passengers and waving to Kurt, the captain.

"Daphne, is that you?" he said in a teasing voice as she took a middle seat in the hopes of protecting her outfit from the inevitable sea spray. "You look as pretty as a picture tonight. Going somewhere special?"

"I have a date," she said shyly as she spread her dress around her knees and tucked her feet under the chair.

Kurt leaned back, bracing himself against the row of seats in front of her, and gave a nod of approval. "Whoever you're meeting is a lucky man." He smiled at her, though she noticed that his eyes held a hint of sadness. "With your hair done up like that, you look just like my wife. She was a beauty too. May the good Lord rest her soul," he added, removing his captain's hat before bowing his head low.

"I know you miss her." Daphne leaned forward to grip his hand. Kurt had been married to Lottie for thirty-five years before she passed, and the entire island had turned up for her funeral service. The eulogy he had given in his wife's honor had brought the entire church to tears, and at the time, Daphne remembered hoping that someday she too would find a love like that.

"Every day of my life." Kurt returned the hat to his head and patted her arm. "I'd love to stay and chat, but I'd better get behind that wheel if I'm going to deliver you to your date on time." He released her, then greeted the other passengers as they took their seats before slipping into his seat behind the wheel and guiding the ferry into the waves.

The trip passed quickly—more quickly than Daphne would have liked, given that her nerves were now shooting through the roof—and before she knew it, she was stepping onto solid ground once more. A short taxi ride to the restaurant followed, and after Daphne thanked the driver, she gazed at the front door, which was adorned with soft fairy lights that immediately evoked a romantic ambience. She hesitated before opening it, giving herself a few moments to take several deep breaths to calm her nerves, and then she smoothed her hair back one last time before entering the restaurant.

More fairy lights hung from the walls, and soft music was flowing out from the overhead speakers. It was an intimate space, with small tables set for two sprinkled around the cozy room, and waiters in bow ties and jackets bustling around carrying trays and bottles of wine. The patrons were almost exclusively couples—some holding hands across their table, some conversing quietly as they enjoyed their meals, some leaning in to whisper into each other's ears. Daphne immediately felt out of place, although she did her best to hide it as she tucked her purse under her arm and greeted the host.

"Good evening, madame," he said, smiling at her. "Do you have a reservation?"

"Yes. Under the name Corinne?" Daphne glanced around the restaurant, her eyes seeking out a man seated by himself, but before she could scan the entire room, the host interrupted her.

"Ah, yes, here we go. Table for two? Your party has already arrived and asked me to escort you to him." The host stepped out from behind his podium and straightened his suit jacket. "If you'll follow me, madame."

They wove through the tables, heading for the far corner of the restaurant, and Daphne's heart leapt into her throat as they approached a man seated with his back to them. He had golden-blond hair and broad shoulders, and he was wearing a well-cut gray sport jacket and dark jeans. A bottle of champagne was already chilling on the table, but the glasses were left untouched—a gentleman's move, Daphne thought as she thanked the host and rounded the table to greet her date.

The man stood when he saw her, and then his mouth dropped open.

"Daphne?" he said in surprise, and then he laughed, his eyes glimmering in the dim lighting. "Are you my mystery date?"

"The one and only." Daphne felt the tension melting from her body as she looked up into the man's familiar face—although she wasn't sure whether to be thrilled or disappointed. "I'd say it's been a long time, Luke, but..." She made a show of playfully checking her watch. "I think I saw you at the inn a few hours ago." She laughed. "Why didn't you mention you had a date?"

Tana had hired Luke Showalter to oversee the renovations to her uncle's inn, and he and Daphne had been acquainted for years. She was also surprised to see him on a date in the first place—it was the island's worst-kept secret that he'd never gotten over the divorce from his former wife, Lydia.

Luke shrugged, grinning at her good-naturedly. "It's strange enough to be set up on a blind date. I didn't want to broadcast it to the entire island, too. You know what people can be like…"

"Nosy," Daphne supplied. "Which is why I only told Tana."

She settled into the chair Luke had pulled out for her and folded her hands on the table, giving him a curious look. "But what I don't understand is how you know my sister, Corinne. She hasn't lived on the island in two decades."

Luke shook his head. "I had no idea Corinne was your sister. I did some work on her house a few months ago. She spent half the time hovering around me, trying to subtly find out whether I had a wife. I thought she was asking for herself—I felt so sorry for her poor husband." He chuckled. "I guess she was trying to see if I'd be good for *you*."

His eyes roamed over her face for a brief moment, soft and inquisitive, and Daphne could feel her cheeks heating. Fortunately, the waiter chose that moment to approach them with their menus, and the topic quickly turned to the restaurant's delicious entrée options. After they placed their order, Luke uncorked the champagne, and they toasted to the surprising turn of events before he guided the conversation back to her.

"So a little bird tells me that you're going to be

the official baker for the inn once it opens again," he said, spreading butter on a slice of bread as Daphne did the same. "That sounds like an exciting opportunity."

"It was." Daphne took a sip of her champagne, smiling at him over the rim of her glass. "But then Henry decided he wanted to offer his guests a full breakfast again, and since I'm not a chef, I'm out."

"Ouch." Luke winced. "I'm sorry for mentioning it—I didn't know."

"It's not all bad news," Daphne said, trailing her fingertip along a drop of champagne that had spilled on the white tablecloth. "Tana's brother Jax is going to be the temporary chef, and in a few months, he's going to train me to be his replacement. He was a renowned chef in Philadelphia who had his own restaurant, so I'll be in good hands."

Her last words were spoken with such conviction that she'd almost convinced herself they were true.

"A chef, huh?" Luke leaned back in his chair, folding his arms over his broad chest and studying her face. "That sounds like a good opportunity." But she could hear the question behind his words, almost as if he'd picked up on something she'd left unspoken. "Is that what you want?"

Daphne sighed. "Yes and no. It's a good opportunity, like you said—better than what Henry originally hired me for. And it will allow me to quit my job at the diner much sooner than I would have otherwise. But if I really think about what I want out of life, out of my career..." She hesitated, letting the rest of the sentence linger in the air between them, unfinished.

Luke leaned forward, resting his elbows on the table as he gazed at her intently. "It's not that," he finished, his voice low as another couple passed by them.

Daphne twisted the napkin in her lap into a ball before finally nodding. "I feel bad for even thinking that—Tana has gone out of her way to try and help me, and I feel like not accepting her offer would be a slap in the face."

Luke shook his head, then grabbed the bottle of champagne and poured more into each of their glasses. "No offense, but I think you have it completely wrong."

Daphne accepted her champagne glass but frowned at his blunt words. "You think so?"

"I do." Luke crossed his arms over his chest, still regarding her steadily. "I've gotten to know Tana pretty well over the past few weeks, and I can tell she has a good heart. If she offered to help you, it's because she wants you to be happy, and that means she won't mind if you turn down her job offer."

He broke off another piece of bread, chewing it while he regarded Daphne thoughtfully. "So tell me —if you could do anything in the world, anything at all... what would it be?"

"I would open up a bakery of my own," Daphne answered without hesitation. She'd never voiced her dreams out loud to anyone before, but in the quiet of the night, when she sat on the beach and gazed out at the dark water, envisioning her future, the images always looked the same.

Luke spread his hands wide and grinned at her. "Knowing what you want is the first step. So why don't you make it happen?"

"A lack of confidence, I guess." Daphne laughed. "And a lack of funds. I can't imagine what it would cost to start a bakery of my own—the rent, the equipment, the ingredients..." The list went on and on, and the more Daphne tallied up a quick total in her head, the more disheartened she became.

Luke, noticing the sudden slump to her shoulders, reached across the table and rested his hand lightly over hers. "It's easy to get bogged down in the details and the worries and the fears. The hard thing is setting those aside, believing in yourself, and taking what you want out of life. Before I started my business, I had all the same doubts as you. But I knew that the more time I wasted fearing the unknown, the less time I had left to be doing what I loved every day. Have you ever sat down, done some research, and crunched the numbers? It might be doable—you can dip into your nest egg and then get a small business loan to fund the rest. Then, you'll get started, you'll work hard, and in a year from now, two years, five... who knows where you might be?"

He smiled at her. "It's hard to trust in yourself and your abilities—believe me, I know. But sometimes we have to bet on ourselves, and the outcome can be better than our wildest dreams."

When he was finished speaking, Daphne allowed her mind to wander for a few moments—and as she had so many times before, she pictured herself behind the counter of a small bakery, selling her homemade cupcakes, pies, and cookies to the island's residents and visitors. She had no doubt that a bakery could be successful in Dolphin Bay—she couldn't count the number of times the tourists she waited on at the diner asked where they could find one. But could it be successful with *her* at the helm?

"Yes."

Once again, Luke seemed to be reading her mind. When she glanced up, he was grinning at her over the rim of his champagne glass.

"If you're asking yourself whether you can really do it, then my answer is yes. You're smart, and you're tenacious, and you're a hard worker. Not only that, but since you've worked at the diner for so many years, everyone on the island knows you by name. You know the kind of community Dolphin Bay is, how everyone here takes care of their own. Do you really think we wouldn't support you?"

He picked up a breadstick and pointed it at her. "If you do this, I'll be your first customer. And that's a promise."

CHAPTER 12

"*I* need to talk to you."

Tana glanced up from her book, looking taken aback by Jax's grave tone. "Sure. Is everything okay?"

She slid a bookmark between the pages and flipped the book shut before setting it on the small table beside her. Then she folded her hands in her lap and gave him an expectant look that was part worry, part curiosity.

Jax swallowed hard. He had been dreading this moment, but at the same time, he knew he had no other choice. He had to tell his sister what he saw when he walked into Reed's apartment last night, even though he had spent most of the day trying to figure some way out of it. The idea of sitting beside her, watching her heart break in two—again—was almost more than he could bear.

He stared down at his hands. "This is hard for me to say, but—"

"It's okay, I already know something's up."

Tana patted the wicker chair beside her, gesturing for Jax to sit down. He stared at her in bewilderment as he lowered himself to the chair, which squawked in protest under his weight, and noted that his sister's eyes were filled with concern —for him.

Tana sighed heavily as she took Jax's hand and gave it a gentle squeeze. "We may not have seen too much of each other over the past few years, but you're still my brother, and I love you. Ever since you stepped foot on the island, I can tell that something's troubling you."

When he opened his mouth to protest this abrupt turn in the conversation, she held up her hand and said, "I know, I know, you lost your restaurant and that's devastating, of course. But there's something else going on with you. I can feel it, and I want to help you—I can only do that, though, if you'll let me."

When their gazes met, Jax felt something inside him break. He had kept the truth about himself hidden from Tana—and everyone else—for so long, but at what cost? He had been silently suffering for years; every moment of his life had been shaped by the secrets that were weighing him down, suffocating him. He had lost everything, and he'd had to work tirelessly to rebuild his life, brick by brick, until it had all come crashing down around him once more, this time through no fault of his own.

But was the first time really his fault? He had been a scared, lonely kid, and he had gotten in over his head. He had managed to claw his way back to the surface, but maybe it was time, finally, to unburden himself from the past once and for all.

Tana was still watching him, her gaze steady on his face, and he could feel the raw grief he'd been holding at bay surging to the surface. He whiteknuckled the arms of his chair and leaned his head back against the worn pillow before squeezing his eyes shut and letting out a ragged sigh.

It was a vulnerable moment made worse by the memory that always plagued him when he allowed his mind to wander back to those days—the image of Daphne, standing at the Dolphin Bay harbor, her long blonde hair blowing around her beautiful face as she waved goodbye to him while the ferry churned away. She looked sad, but hopeful too—and excited, for the future he had promised her. It was a promise he had intended to keep. On that warm end-of-summer day, when the sun was bright and the blue sky was endless, Jax had no idea he wouldn't see her face again for more than two decades.

He had no idea she would end up hating him as the life that should have been theirs lay scattered and broken at their feet.

His face twisted in pain as the memory faded away, replaced by the hard, unforgiving look in her eyes the last time he had seen her.

"Tell me," Tana whispered. "Please, Jax—tell me what's going on. Let me help you."

Jax stared hard at his hands, willing Daphne's face to go away. When it finally did, he slumped back in his chair and covered his eyes with trembling fingers. "Okay," he said, taking a deep breath. "Okay. I guess it's time I finally told someone."

Tana's eyes flashed with fear, and he realized that, from an outsider's perspective, he must have looked like he was about to drop terrible news. "It's fine," he said gently, composing himself and straightening back up in his chair. "It's old news, Tana, but it's a burden I've been carrying for a long time."

His sister gave a shaky laugh and pressed her hand to her chest. "You're scaring me, Jax. Are you sick? Hurt?"

"No," Jax said quickly, and then pursed his lips, reconsidering. "Not anymore." He nodded toward the glass of lemonade sitting on the table beside Tana. "Can I?"

She nodded mutely and handed it to him, watching as he drained the entire glass in one long gulp. "My goodness," she said, eyes wide as he passed the empty glass back to her. "Should I get something stronger?"

Jax's wince was automatic, but he knew that Tana's words, however unintentional, were also a starting point. "No, you shouldn't—and I guess that's where this story begins."

He leaned forward, resting his elbows on his knees and steepling his fingers beneath his chin as he stared out over the serene blue-gray waters surrounding the island. The sun was setting in a pink-streaked sky, and in the distance, he could see the ferry gliding toward the harbor as a trio of seagulls circled overhead. "The story begins here, on the island, but before then, too. With Mom."

He glanced at his sister, who was frowning as she kept her gaze steady on his face. He laughed lightly, though the sound held no happiness. "From the time we were young, I always felt so unsettled, so... unwanted, I guess you could say." He watched a dolphin slip in and out of the waves and pictured himself as a boy, watching his mother pack yet another suitcase before dropping him and Tana off at a relative's house. "I'm not sure Mom ever wanted kids, you know? I felt—and I still feel now—that we were nothing more than a burden to her. An afterthought, something unpleasant to be dealt with."

Tana nodded and gave him a tight smile. "I feel the same way. It's taken me a long time to get over that. I keep my distance from her for a reason."

Jax ran a frustrated hand through his hair. "But no matter how many times she shipped us off to one house or another, you were always that happy-go-lucky, sunny kid. It never seemed to bother you—"

"I wouldn't go that far," Tana interrupted, shaking her head. "Why do you think I never really visited Dolphin Bay after I went to college? I told myself I was busy, but the reality was, there were a lot of hurt feelings tied up in this place. Part of me was dreading coming back here, maybe for that very reason. Now that I'm here, though, I've realized that I'm able to separate the two. The island was never at fault. Mom was."

"Yeah, she was." Jax's voice drifted off as he considered Tana's words. He'd never realized that she'd been hurt, too—she'd never let it show. The idea of that brought him no peace, though. In fact, it only reinforced what he had known all along: that he was broken.

"But it went beyond hurt feelings for me, sis. Way, way beyond that. I couldn't cope. Every summer, being back in this place, knowing she was dumping us on Uncle Henry, who probably didn't want to be bothered... it just wrecked me. Eventually, I figured out that there was a way to numb the pain."

By now, his hands were clenched so tightly in his lap that the skin on his knuckles was stretched to its limits. His next words were a whisper that prompted Tana to lean sideways in her chair to hear him.

"I started drinking, and once that happened, I couldn't stop. It got worse, and worse, and by the time I was eighteen, I had completely lost control. That last summer on the island—" He took a deep breath and closed his eyes against the pain. "Things were bad. I was in a fight for my life, Tana. If I kept doing what I was doing, I was literally going to die. A doctor on the mainland confirmed it."

His sister's eyes were filled with tears now, but she didn't bother wiping them away. Instead, she gripped his hand and continued listening as Jax bowed his head. "When summer was over and I left the island, you and Mom both thought that I was in college. The reality was, I had hit rock bottom. I entered myself into a treatment facility. I was there for six months. And when I got out, I thought I would be better, I thought I would be fixed. But the real struggle was just beginning."

He stared at her with imploring eyes, willing her to understand. "I had to leave everything about my old life behind. I needed to start fresh. The idea of stepping foot on the island again, going back to the way things were… it was too much. There is no doubt in my mind that it would have killed me. So I left the island, and I never came back. And I left her too. I didn't even say goodbye, because I couldn't."

He slumped against the chair, finally unburdened from the weight of silence that had been crushing him for so many years. Long minutes passed, and when he finally looked up and met his sister's gaze, he saw a face that was filled with warmth and compassion and, most importantly, acceptance.

"Thank you," he said quietly, toying with the hem of his shirt. "For listening."

"Thank you for sharing." Tana rose from her chair and pulled Jax into a long hug. He buried his face in her shoulder, and they stood like that for a long time, until finally, she broke the embrace and stepped back from him. She wiped at her eyes with the sleeve of her blouse, and then said, "I had no idea. I wish you had known that you could have confided in me then, but I'm glad you were able to now."

"I couldn't." Jax felt his throat constrict. "But it's been a long time, and I guess I finally have the strength to tell you now."

"And being back on the island? It hasn't harmed you?" Tana's voice was anxious as she took her seat again.

Jax shook his head. "No. I was positive that it would, but I had no choice—I had to come back, or else I'd be out on the streets. But like you said, being back here now, after so many years—"

He paused to watch two young children laughing as they galloped around on the sand below, one clutching the string of a kite shaped like a dragon. "I guess what they say is true. Time heals all wounds. I'm able to see the beauty and serenity of the island in a way I never could before. That being said, I'm not sure if I can stay here long-term. But at least for now… I'm safe."

Tana nodded, following her brother's gaze to the beach. For a time, they watched the children run along the water, their kite soaring after them, until a woman—their mother, presumably—called to them from the sand.

"There's one thing you told me that I'm not quite sure I understand, though." She turned her head to meet Jax's eyes. "You said you left the island, and you left *her*. Who are you talking about?"

Jax exhaled softly, his head falling back to rest against the chair. "Daphne," he said, his voice low. "I'm talking about Daphne."

~

TANA LISTENED in shock for the next few minutes as her brother told her about the secret romance that had blossomed between him and Daphne during those summer days and nights spent exploring the island's shores. She searched her memory, trying to remember something, *anything*, that she had missed—a shared look, a private joke, a flirtatious hand on the arm. But there had been nothing.

Part of her felt hurt that they had kept their relationship from her—she was close with her brother, and considered Daphne to be her best friend. But another part of her understood. Summer romances were fragile, and teenage love even more so—hold it the wrong way, and it could break.

And break it did. Along with Tana's own heart, for both of them.

"You need to explain all of this to her," she said, her voice filled with conviction.

"I know." Jax had been staring at his hands for the past few minutes, clenching and unclenching his fists. "I just haven't been able to bring myself to do it. Every time I see her, I start to work up the nerve, but she's just so angry with me. I figure sometimes it's better to let sleeping dogs lie." He gave her a desperate look. "Wouldn't dredging up the past, making her relive everything that happened between us, only make things worse?"

"No," Tana said firmly. "Daphne deserves to know the truth so she can move on. So she can decide what type of relationship, if any, she wants to have with you going forward." She blew out a long breath. "Obviously I never would have suggested that the two of you work together if I had known what had happened. I feel like an idiot."

"Frankly, I'm surprised Daphne never told you." Jax shook his head, and Tana could see the strain on every line of his face. He let out a bitter laugh. "You should have seen the look on her face when she stopped by the inn to see you only to find me here instead. But when I saw her… it was almost like twenty-five years fell away in the blink of an eye."

He stared out over the water, his eyes following the movement of a group of teenagers tossing a ball around in the shallow waves. "We were like them once," he murmured. "Our whole lives stretched ahead of us. We thought we'd have things figured out by now." He snorted and shook his head again. "Guess we were wrong."

"Guess we were," Tana replied, studying her brother's profile. "Jax," she said gently, and then waited for him to turn toward her. When he did, his eyes were filled with pain. "Are you still in love with her?"

He was quiet for a long moment after that, returning his gaze to the sea, his shoulders hunched as he sat forward in the chair, his hands clasped together. Finally, he said, "I don't know. When we were kids, I knew in every bone of my body that she was the one. Giving her up was like losing a limb— like someone was physically tearing me apart."

He ran his fingers down the days-old stubble on his cheeks. "But if I didn't, what kind of life would I have offered her? She was already being held hostage by her mother's drinking; was I really going to add to her pain? In letting her go, I saved myself—but I also saved her from a lifetime of misery." His voice was filled with such longing that Tana's heart ached for him, for what might have been.

They fell into silence once more after that, the sound broken only by the distant crashing of the waves against the shore and the shouts of the teenagers as they packed up their things for the evening and traipsed through the sand. Tana watched them, thinking about what Jax had said. When she was a teenager, she couldn't wait to grow older, to experience everything that adult life had to offer. And now that she was an adult, with the pressures and heartaches and responsibilities that came with it, what wouldn't she give to be young and carefree again?

Her thoughts drifted to her daughter Emery, now out on her own, soaking in the excitement of the big city. What cards would life deal to her, and more importantly, had Tana and Derek prepared her to handle whatever was thrown her way? Her own mother had taken little interest in nurturing her children, in teaching them the ways of the world and what to expect out of life—the good and the bad— and in many ways that absence had shaped Tana's view of the world.

And it had shaped Jax too, for better or for worse. Yes, he'd suffered tremendously from it, but he'd also developed a tenacity and self-sufficiency that had served him well, and would continue to do so long into the future. Her brother had no idea how strong he really was.

"Things will be okay," she said, reaching for his hand. "You'll see." She gestured to herself. "Look at me. A few months ago, things had reached a breaking point. But now..." She smiled softly. "Life is starting to look better than ever."

Jax blinked at her, as if trying to make sense of her words, and then suddenly, he shot up in his chair, a look of horror dawning on his face. "Tana, I forgot that I was supposed to tell—"

The sound of footsteps crunching on gravel reached their ears, and Jax and Tana turned to find Reed walking across the inn's driveway, shielding his eyes against the last, powerful rays of the setting sun. Jax half-stood from his chair, looking stricken, and Tana frowned at her brother as she rose to greet Reed.

"Hi," she murmured, pressing a soft kiss to his cheek and taking his hand. "I'm so glad you're here— I was just thinking about you." She gestured toward the porch. "Would you like to join us? I can put a kettle on the stove and we can watch what's left of the sunset."

"That sounds nice," Reed said, glancing over her shoulder at Jax. "But first, do you think you and I could take a walk on the beach? There's something I'd like to discuss with you."

His words left Tana feeling uneasy, but his expression was neutral, and so she nodded and said, "Lead the way," before informing Jax of their plans. Her brother merely gave a brief nod in response, but his eyes followed them as they crossed the driveway and headed for the winding dirt path that led down to the sand. As they walked, Reed reached for Tana's hand, and she slipped it into his, their fingers interlacing as naturally as if they were meant to fit together.

"How was your day?" she asked as they stepped to the side of the path to allow a family with three young children to trudge past them, their arms weighed down with beach gear.

"Long," he said as they continued walking. "I couldn't wait to see you. I missed you terribly."

When they reached the end of the path, he released her hand, then led her to their favorite spot near the water. They sat side by side, their shoulders touching, and Tana kicked off her shoes and wiggled her toes in the soft sand with a happy sigh.

"I'm not sure life could get any better than this," she said, her eyes on a speedboat cutting a path through the waves as it headed back to the harbor.

Reed was silent for a long moment, his face turned toward the sea, and then he shifted his entire body toward her and took both of her hands in his. "Something happened last night that I want you to know about." He inhaled deeply and gazed into her eyes, his expression serious, before he continued.

"Kelly, my assistant, stopped by my apartment under the pretense of turning in her notice. Somehow, she got it in her head that I would only pursue a romantic relationship with her if we were no longer working together." He shook his head, his mouth twisting into a wry smile. "I'm not sure I could have made my feelings—or lack of feelings, I should say—any more clear, but that didn't stop her from kissing me. As soon as I realized what was happening, I immediately broke the kiss, of course, and told her to leave."

Tana felt her breath catch as she imagined the two of them together, alone in Reed's apartment, Kelly's arms around his neck and his hands tangled in her hair. It was an all-too-familiar nightmare, one she had been picturing since the day she realized her feelings for Reed were strong. After all, it had happened with Derek—and after more than twenty years of marriage, no less. Reed, by comparison, was a virtual stranger.

She supposed she should have expected this to happen. Fool me once, and so on.

Happiness was elusive. When things seemed too good to be true, they usually were. Reed may have told Kelly to leave last night out of a sense of loyalty to Tana, but in time, he would realize that—

"—in love with you."

She blinked, realizing that Reed was still speaking, and turned to him with a frown. "What did you say?"

Reed's pale blue eyes were sparkling in the last rays of the fading sunlight, and a gentle smile was playing across his handsome face. He took her hands once more, giving them a squeeze before raising them to his lips, turning them over, and pressing a kiss to each palm. "I told her that I was falling in love with you."

Tana stared back at him, speechless.

"And I am, Tana, with my whole heart." He brushed a strand of hair back from her face, then cupped her chin in his hand. "I don't expect you to tell me you feel the same way—in fact, I don't want you to say that, not until you're sure. *If* you're ever sure." His gaze remained steady on hers. "You have a lot going on in your life right now, and I respect that. But I needed you to know how I felt."

When he had finished speaking, Tana realized she had been holding her breath. She let it out now in a whoosh as she tried to wrap her mind around the things he was saying to her. Mere moments ago, she was envisioning the end of their relationship. And now, he was telling her that it was just the beginning.

But did she want this?

A new life, a different life, was waiting for her; all she needed to do was reach out and grab it.

A wave of sadness washed over her as she pictured her and Derek growing old together, holding hands as they walked on a California beach, watching their grandchildren playing nearby in the sand. Emery was there too, her dark hair whipping around her head as she ran along the sand with her children. This was the family she was supposed to have—everyone together, forever.

But some dreams were never meant to be. They were bent and broken and battered, but then, in time, something different emerged from the ashes of what might have been.

Something different, but just as beautiful.

Now she could envision a new future, where she and Reed walked along the shore, their hands entwined, the silhouette of the inn behind them as they watched the island's breathtaking sunset before returning to the home, the life, they'd built together.

It was all in front of her, so close she could practically trace her finger along its edges.

Reed was no longer watching her. He had left her alone with her thoughts as he gazed out over the dusky purple sky. His hand was hanging loosely at his side, and she stared at it for a moment as past and present collided in her mind, as the months of what-might-have-beens morphed into a future of what-could-be.

And then she leaned forward and reached for his hand.

CHAPTER 13

"I'm just not sure I can swing it." Daphne groaned with frustration and rested her head in her hands, taking a moment to ignore the bank statements and loan applications and other paperwork scattered on the floor around her. She'd spent the past three days completely immersed in research on how to start a small business, even taking time off from her job at the diner—a true rarity—to focus on it.

"You can. You absolutely can." Luke took a swig from his can of soda, then set it down on the floor and picked up the bank statement, waving it playfully in Daphne's direction. "You have way more in savings than I did when I got started with my business, and think of all the equipment I had to buy just to make myself look like the real deal." He shuddered. "I can't tell you how many sleepless nights I had, sweating it out before I booked that first job."

Daphne groaned again. "Great, thanks, that's just what I needed to hear." She grabbed the loan application, preparing to tear it in half. "This was a stupid idea. I can't possibly—"

"The point is," Luke said, tugging the application out of her hand, "I *did* book that first job. And then the second, and the third. Now, ten years later, I couldn't tell you the number of clients I've worked with."

He smoothed the paper out on the floor, then handed it back to Daphne. "When you finally open the doors to your very own bakery, I guarantee on the first day—heck, for the first *year*—you're going to count the number of people who walk through them. But then, eventually, you'll lose count. Because it won't matter anymore. You'll be doing the thing you love, and it'll be hard work, but all the blood, sweat, tears, and terrifyingly empty bank accounts will be worth it. I promise you that."

Daphne raised her head from her hands once more as she considered Luke's words. Here he was, a successful businessman—and more importantly, a friend—who was encouraging her to go for it, because he believed in her. The trouble was, no matter which way she looked at it, Daphne was having a hard time believing in herself. And until she did that, she would never succeed.

But what was the alternative? Did she really want to wait tables at the diner forever?

"Come on, come on, you're almost there." Luke's eyes sparkled playfully as he beckoned toward her. "Just imagine yourself mere *months* from now, standing behind the counter and serving customers at your very own bakery. Imagine them raving about your delicious cakes, and telling all their friends to order one. Imagine—"

"Okay, okay." Daphne held up her hands to stop him, laughing while also shaking her head in disbelief. "I can't believe I'm going to do this. I can't believe you're actually convincing me to do this."

"I'm not." Luke shrugged, then reached for the plate of chocolate chip cookies beside him on the floor. "I'm just telling you what you already know— this is your future. You just need to pull the trigger. Besides," he added, waving another cookie in her direction, "I need more of this in my life. You would be doing the entire island a disservice if you stayed at Sal's."

"Somehow I don't think Sal is going to see it that way." She could already picture her boss's reaction when she told him that she was hanging up her apron forever. Sal's already red face would quickly resemble an overripe tomato, and he would start waving his hands frantically in the air as he rattled off all the reasons she should stay.

But she wouldn't be swayed. She couldn't. Because she had a reason to leave, and it was the most important one of all.

"I'm going to do it." She took a deep breath, then let it out and gave a shaky laugh as she grabbed the loan application off the floor, along with a pen. "I'm forty-three years old. It's time I followed my dreams." She gave Luke, whose cheeks were still bulging with cookies, an anxious look. "Will you still be my first customer?"

He swallowed, and then grinned at her. "If you keep making treats like these, I can assure you, Daphne—you won't be able to get rid of me."

~

A FEW WEEKS LATER, a slightly nauseous Daphne was standing outside a vacant storefront in the heart of downtown Dolphin Bay, Luke at her side.

"This looks perfect," he said, cupping his hands around his eyes to peer through the window. "It used to be Lisa Welling's coffee shop before she got married and moved to the mainland—look! It even has a counter and display case installed." He turned to Daphne, his eyes shining with excitement. "This might be the one."

Daphne smiled back at him, touched by his helpfulness—not to mention his boundless energy and enthusiasm. After reflecting on the advice he had given her during their surprise blind date, she had contacted him the next morning to ask if he would help guide her as she started the process of determining whether she would really take the plunge and build a business of her own.

He had readily and happily agreed, and for the past few weeks, he had been by her side as she spoke to loan officers and made countless spreadsheets and researched the ins and outs of the bakery business late into the night, her eyes bleary as she stared at her computer, a mug of lukewarm coffee by her side. He had even taken it upon himself to call local realtors to see if anyone had a rental property that was within her budget—and lo and behold, a potential deal had fallen through just a few days ago, leaving the former coffee shop available… and for a much more reasonable monthly cost than Daphne could have ever imagined.

Daphne knew she would never be able to pay him back for his kindness. As she watched him now, eagerly pressing his nose to the glass, she was unable to ignore the fluttering feeling in her stomach, the one that had been growing more insistent as each day passed. Luke Showalter was a gem of a man, and even though she was loath to admit it, she was glad that Corinne had convinced her to go out on a limb and meet someone new.

Or in this case, an old friend who maybe, just maybe, could become something more.

"Hi, you must be Daphne."

A woman in a dark gray business suit approached them, a set of keys dangling from her hand. She shook Daphne's hand, then turned to Luke and did the same before sorting through the keys and inserting a small gold one into the shop's front door lock.

As she pushed open the door, she said, "I understand you're interested in opening a bakery? We have several available rental properties in Dolphin

Bay, but I think this one is best suited to your purposes. It also has a fantastic location—the owner of the coffee shop that used to be here did a brisk business before she moved." The realtor waved her hand toward the window, where a steady stream of people passed by, glancing inside with interest before moving to the next shop.

Luke unfolded a piece of paper that contained the list of questions he and Daphne had prepared, but as he and the realtor began speaking, Daphne barely listened. She was too busy wandering around the cozy space, her fingers trailing along the front of the display case as she imagined it stuffed to the brim with the cookies, cakes, pies, and other pastries whose recipes she'd worked to perfect in her own kitchen over the years. She could picture her fellow islanders stopping by first thing in the morning for a cup of freshly brewed coffee and a donut, or meeting with her at one of the small tables she'd set up to place an order for a special-occasion cake. Daphne had only recently begun dabbling in cake decorating, but she'd already discovered that she had a knack for it. Why not add wedding cake design to her future plans?

As Luke and the realtor continued their conversation, Daphne made a beeline for the kitchen. To her surprise, it already included several high-quality stainless-steel appliances, including a massive double oven that would allow her to produce her baked goods in large quantities. A huge freestanding freezer stood in the back corner, providing ample storage space, and there was a walk-in pantry that could house all of her ingredients. The entire kitchen was a chef's dream.

Or, in this case, a baker's dream.

Daphne hadn't told Tana her plans yet; she was waiting until she formalized them before letting her know that she would no longer be taking over the job as chef at the inn once Jax stepped down. She was no longer worried about her friend's reaction; she knew Tana would be as wonderful and supportive as ever. And as a bonus, Daphne could avoid working one-on-one with Jax—forever. Although they'd seen each other in passing a handful of times when Daphne stopped by the inn to chat with Tana or discuss business ideas with Luke, she made sure to give him a wide berth. The damage he'd done to her heart may have healed over, but it was still there, a reminder of all that could have been.

"Daphne?" Luke called from the front of the shop a moment before poking his head through the kitchen doorway. When he saw the setup, he whistled appreciatively. "This looks awesome," he said, and when Daphne nodded vigorously in agreement, he gave her a sly smile. "So is this the one?"

Daphne took a deep breath to calm her nerves before spreading her arms wide to encompass the room and grinning at him. "It is. It absolutely is."

"Well then," Luke said, offering her his arm, "what are we waiting for? Let's go tell the realtor the good news."

And together they walked out of the kitchen... and into Daphne's future.

~

LATER THAT EVENING, Daphne was reviewing her rental agreement when someone knocked at the door, soft yet insistent. She slid Luna off her lap and yawned widely, stretching her arms over her head and rotating her hips as her body groaned in protest. Over the past few weeks, she'd spent far too much time hunched over her tiny computer desk, and it was starting to take a toll on her.

Padding over to the door, she slid back the lock while simultaneously peering through the peephole, expecting to see Luke, who'd promised to stop over for a celebratory slice of apple pie and some Netflix binge-watching in honor of Daphne signing the rental agreement that afternoon. So far she and Luke had kept things strictly platonic, although, admittedly, the space between them on the couch was shrinking as the weeks ticked by. He was a sweetheart of a man, charming and warm-hearted, the kind of man a girl could find herself falling in love with if she wasn't careful.

The visitor's head was bent, obscuring his face from her view, but instead of Luke's blond hair, she saw a much darker shade—and then the man lifted his face, and his blue-green eyes latched onto hers through the peephole.

She backed up a step, her heartrate kicking up, her traitorous pulse racing as it did every time she saw him. Time and heartache hadn't dimmed the effect he had on her; the effect he'd perhaps always have.

Daphne took a few moments to compose herself before opening the door. "What are you doing here?" she asked in lieu of a greeting.

Jax's hands were shoved deep in his pockets, his face darkened by the shadows cast down from the cloud-covered moon. "Can I talk to you for a few minutes?" he asked, his eyes lowered to the ground.

Then he inhaled sharply and raised them to her face. "Please."

"I'm not sure that's such a good idea." Daphne crossed her arms over her chest and glanced out the door, hoping to see Luke walking down the street toward her apartment. If ever there was a good time for an interruption, this was it.

"Daphne—please. I'm only asking for five minutes of your time, and then you'll never have to speak to me again." His voice was pleading, and a portion of Daphne's resolve cracked.

"Fine," she said, heaving a sigh and flinging the door open before stepping back to allow him entry to her apartment. He gave her a grateful nod, then followed her to the couch. He sank down onto it and then perched nervously on the edge of the cushion while she immediately crossed the room, heading for the furthest armchair, and huddled into it, pulling an old hand-knitted blanket over her lap and toying with its fraying edges to avoid meeting his gaze.

The silence hung heavily in the air between them as Jax stared at his hands, flexing and unflexing his fingers, before he finally said, "I owe you an explanation."

Daphne turned her face away from him to avoid

meeting his eyes. "You're about twenty-five years too late for that, Jax."

He nodded. "I know." Then he rubbed his palms along the length of his thighs and added, "But that doesn't mean you don't deserve one now."

Daphne was gripping the blanket now, twisting the fabric until it threatened to tear, and then she forced herself to relax her hands. She didn't want him to know the effect his presence was having on her—she didn't want to give him the satisfaction of knowing that somewhere inside her, maybe not as deep down as she believed, she still cared.

"Okay," she finally bit out, turning a glare in his direction. "Spit it out."

Jax winced, but quickly covered it with a tight smile. "I'll be quick," he said. "I promise." And then he gave a humorless laugh. "Not that my promises mean much in your book."

The tears were threatening to form then, and Daphne blinked them back rapidly, lowering her gaze to the blanket so he wouldn't notice. She kept her eyes pinned to her lap as he took a deep breath and began to speak, and even though she wouldn't look at him, she could feel his gaze on her face like a hot brand.

"There's something you don't know about me—

or you didn't know about me back when we were together." He swallowed hard. "I was keeping the truth hidden from everyone, even myself, for a long, long time." He paused, as if collecting himself, before forging on. "You know I had some... difficulties... with my relationship with my mother growing up, about how she always seemed to pawn Tana and me off on whoever was around instead of actually taking the time to raise us herself?"

He paused again, waiting for a reaction, and Daphne gave a grudging nod. It was one of the first things they had bonded over, back then, but that was before Daphne's own mother had taken her final turn for the worse, before she entered the point of no return.

Softly, he continued, "That had a bigger effect on me than I was willing to admit, and eventually, to numb the pain, I started drinking."

At this, Daphne raised her eyes to stare at him, but when their gazes met, he looked away. "I was ashamed of what I was doing, at how bad it got, but I also needed it. It was like air to me, Daphne. I couldn't breathe without it." He clenched his hands into fists and took another deep breath. "Those last few months on the island, there were times when the pain—when the alcohol—was so all-consuming that

I drank myself into a near-coma each night, just so I wouldn't have to feel any longer."

He raised his head, and their eyes met. "But you," he whispered. "You were my beautiful savior, the only thing that was keeping me tethered to this world. I adored you, Daphne, but..." His voice caught, and he exhaled slowly as he studied his trembling hands. "But I saw what was happening in your life, with your mother, and I couldn't add myself as another burden on your shoulders. And on top of that, if I kept living the way I was, there is no doubt in my mind that I wouldn't have made it to my twenty-first birthday. One night, when things were so bad I could barely stand myself anymore, I decided that I wanted to live. I wanted to have a full life. And so when I said goodbye to you at the harbor and promised you I would be back..."

He looked up, his eyes tortured. "You remember that night, don't you?"

Daphne managed to give a brief nod, her gaze never leaving his face. Of course she remembered that night. It had tormented her for years to come. Perhaps it still did.

"When I said I'd be back for you, I meant it. What you didn't know was that when I stepped off the ferry on the mainland, I took a cab straight to a treatment facility. I was there for months, and when I got out, the thought of going back to the island…"

He squeezed his eyes shut and shook his head. "I knew I would die if I did. I knew I would slip back into my old habits, and this time, there would be no recovering from them. So I left you behind." His voice was a whisper now, his face screwed up in pain. "I left you behind to save myself, but to save you too. Because I refused to make your life any harder than it already was. You were strong, and I knew you would move on. I wasn't nearly as strong, so I stayed away from the island for twenty-five years. I stayed away from you, out of necessity. And I'm sorry, Daphne. I'm so, so sorry."

He clasped his hands in front of his chest. "You were the love of my life, and I gave you up. If it makes you feel any better, I've regretted what I had to do every day of my life. I've never forgiven myself, and I don't expect you to forgive me either. But… I just needed you to understand."

He stood up from the couch. "I'll go now. I don't want to take up any more of your time. Thanks for listening."

Daphne watched him walk toward the door, her eyes welling with tears, her lungs constricting painfully as she tried to take in everything he had told her. A hundred thoughts were racing through her mind at once, all competing for attention, but one question stood out from the rest, stark and sharp as a knife.

How could she not have known?

How could she not have seen what was happening? She searched every corner of her memory, trying to recall a slip of the tongue, a day when he hadn't seemed like himself, a moment when she'd brushed off her suspicions about something that seemed amiss. But nothing came to mind except the sunny, carefree, easygoing boy she had known and loved for most of her childhood. She had no idea the pain that lurked beneath the surface. If she had, she would have done anything—*anything*—to help.

Rising from her chair, she crossed the room swiftly and stopped him at the front door with a hand on his wrist. When he turned to her, his eyes dull, she stepped forward, took his hand, and pulled him into a hug.

He collapsed into her, burying his head in her shoulder, and she let the tears drip freely down her cheeks as she breathed in his familiar scent, the memory of it evoking the sunny days of her youth, the first time—the only time—she had fallen in love. She didn't know how long they stood there, holding each other tight, but eventually, Jax broke the embrace to wipe his eyes with the sleeve of his shirt.

Then he gazed at her, his beautiful eyes bright with unshed tears, and said softly, "Friends?"

Daphne nodded, her throat tight, and gave his hand a gentle squeeze. "Friends."

EPILOGUE

$\mathcal{L}$uke Showalter strolled along the main square, greeting the friends he passed with a warm smile and enjoying the sound of the ocean rolling against the shore. He loved the summer nights on the island—the scents of seawater and funnel cakes mingling in the air, the sounds of children laughing and calling to each other as they explored the boardwalk, the happy couples walking hand in hand along the shore. That last sight always gave him a pang of loneliness, but over the past five years, he had been working hard to move on with his life.

It hadn't been easy. In fact, getting over Lydia—if he could even call it that—was the hardest thing he'd ever had to do.

But tonight, he wouldn't think about that. Tonight, he would be enjoying himself.

After all, things had been going his way for the past few months. He'd been honored to land the job renovating the Inn at Dolphin Bay—the inn was a historic part of the island, a beloved icon, and he took his work on it very seriously. He and his crew were way ahead of schedule, and tomorrow morning, he planned to give Tana and Henry the exciting news that the inn would be ready to open for business again within the next month.

Yes, his professional life was going well.

And it seemed like his personal one might just be turning around too.

He smiled as he thought of Daphne, his unexpected blind date that was blossoming into a wonderful friendship, and perhaps something more. She was a lovely woman, a true catch, and any man would be lucky to have her by his side. Luke was thrilled to be helping her realize her dreams of opening the bakery; he'd struggled on his own path to business ownership, and at the time, he would have been incredibly grateful for a mentor to guide him through the process.

Tonight, they would celebrate the next step she had taken on her journey: signing the rental agreement for a prime shop space right in the town square.

Tonight, once the pie had been eaten and the champagne cork popped, he just might lean in for that kiss.

His phone rang, the upbeat ringtone he'd chosen cutting through his thoughts, and he slid it out of his pocket and answered it without bothering to glance at the caller ID. He'd been fielding calls all day from the subcontractor he'd hired to oversee the installation of the inn's new private guest bathrooms, and just because the clock had ticked past five in the evening didn't mean Luke's job was ever over. It came with the territory.

"Luke here," he said by way of hello, waving to the owner of a bookshop he frequented who was stepping onto the sidewalk to lock up for the night.

There was a long pause, and then a familiar voice, one he hadn't heard in a long time and hoped to never hear again, said, softly and hesitantly, "Luke? It's me."

~

THANK you for reading **The Magic Hour**, the third book in the Dolphin Bay series. Book four, **The Last**

Goodbye, will be available soon, so be sure to sign up for my email list to be the first to know about release day. I'll never share your information with anyone.

To stay connected, check out my Facebook page, send me an email at miakentromance@gmail.com, or visit my website at www.miakent.com. I love to hear from my readers!

And to help indie authors like me continue bringing you the stories you love, please consider leaving a review of this book on the retailer of your choice.

Thank you so much for your support!

Love,

Mia

~

MIA KENT IS the author of clean, contemporary women's fiction and small-town romance. She writes heartfelt stories about love, friendship, happily ever after, and the importance of staying true to yourself.

She's been married for over a decade to her high school sweetheart, and when she isn't working on her next book, she's chasing around a toddler, crawling after an infant, and hiding from an eighty-pound tornado of dog love. Frankly, it's a wonder she writes at all.

To learn more about Mia's books, to sign up for her email list, or to send her a message, visit her website at www.miakent.com.